THE SHORT STORIES OF
LIAM O'FLAHERTY

The Short Stories of Liam O'Flaherty

by Liam O'Flaherty

NEW ENGLISH LIBRARY
TIMES MIRROR

First published in Great Britain by Jonathan Cape Limited in 1937
Reissued 1948

FIRST FOUR SQUARE EDITION NOVEMBER 1966
This abridged NEL edition issued June 1970

NEL Books are published by New English Library Limited, from Barnard's Inn,
Holborn, London, EC1. Made and printed in Great Britain by
Hazell Watson & Viney Ltd, Aylesbury, Bucks

45000546 1

CONTENTS

SPRING SOWING

It was still dark when Martin Delaney and his wife Mary got up. Martin stood in his shirt by the window a long time looking out, rubbing his eyes and yawning, while Mary raked out the live coals that had lain hidden in the ashes on the hearth all night. Outside, cocks were crowing and a white streak was rising from the ground, as it were, and beginning to scatter the darkness. It was a February morning, dry, cold and starry.

The couple sat down to their breakfast of tea, bread and butter, in silence. They had only been married the previous autumn and it was hateful leaving a warm bed at such an early hour. They both felt in a bad humour and ate, wrapped in their thoughts. Martin with his brown hair and eyes, his freckled face and his little fair moustache, looked too young to be married, and his wife looked hardly more than a girl, red-cheeked and blue-eyed, her black hair piled at the rear of her head with a large comb gleaming in the middle of the pile, Spanish fashion. They were both dressed in rough homespuns, and both wore the loose white frieze shirt that Inverara peasants use for work in the fields.

They ate in silence, sleepy and bad humoured and yet on fire with excitement, for it was the first day of their first spring sowing as man and wife. And each felt the glamour of that day on which they were to open up the earth together and plant seeds in it. So they sat in silence and bad humour, for somehow the imminence of an event that had been long expected, loved, feared and prepared for, made them dejected. Mary, with her shrewd woman's mind, munched her bread and butter and thought of ... Oh, what didn't she think of? Of as many things as there are in life does a woman think in the first joy and anxiety of her mating. But Martin's mind was fixed on one thought. Would he be able to prove himself a man worthy of being the head of a family by doing his spring sowing well?

In the barn after breakfast, when they were getting the potato seeds and the line for measuring the ground and the spade, a cross word or two passed between them, and when Martin fell over a basket in the half-darkness of the barn, he swore and said that a man would be better off dead than ... But before he could finish whatever he was going to say, Mary had her arms around his waist and her face to his. 'Martin,' she said, 'let us not begin this day cross with one another.' And there was a tremor in her voice. And somehow, as they embraced and Martin kept mumbling in his awkward peasant's voice, 'pulse of my heart, treasure of my life', and such traditional phrases, all their irritation and sleepiness left them. And they stood there embracing until at last Martin pushed her from him with pretended roughness and said: 'Come, come, girl, it will be sunset before we begin at this rate.'

Still, as they walked silently in their rawhide shoes, through the little hamlet, there was not a soul about. Lights were glimmering in the windows of a few cabins. The sky had a big grey crack in it in the east, as if it were going to burst in order to give birth to the sun. Birds were singing somewhere at a distance. Martin and Mary rested their baskets of seeds on a fence outside the village and Martin whispered to Mary proudly: 'We are first, Mary.' And they both looked back at the little cluster of cabins, that was the centre of their world, with throbbing hearts. For the joy of spring had now taken complete hold of them.

They reached the little field where they were to sow. It was a little triangular patch of ground under an ivy-covered limestone hill. The little field had been manured with seaweed some weeks before, and the weeds had rotted and whitened on the grass. And there was a big red heap of fresh seaweed lying in a corner by the fence to be spread under the seeds as they were laid. Martin, in spite of the cold, threw off everything above his waist except his striped woollen shirt. Then he spat on his hands, seized his spade and cried: 'Now you are going to see what kind of a man you have, Mary.'

'There, now', said Mary, tying a little shawl closer under her chin. 'Aren't we boastful this early hour of the morning? Maybe I'll wait till sunset to see what kind of a man I have got.'

The work began. Martin measured the ground by the southern fence for the first ridge, a strip of ground four feet wide, and he placed the line along the edge and pegged it at each end. Then he spread fresh seaweed over the strip. Mary filled her apron with seeds and began to lay them in rows, four, three, four. When she was a little distance down the ridge Martin advanced with spade to the head eager to commence.

'Now in the name of God', he cried, spitting on his palms, 'let us raise the first sod!'

'Oh, Martin, wait till I'm with you!' cried Mary, dropping her seeds on the ridge and running up to him. Her fingers outside her woollen mittens were numb with the cold, and she couldn't wipe them in her apron. Her cheeks seemed to be on fire. She put an arm round Martin's waist and stood looking at the green sod his spade was going to cut, with the excitement of a little child.

'Now for God's sake, girl, keep back!' said Martin gruffly. 'Suppose anybody saw us trapesing about like this in the field of our spring sowing, what would they take us for but a pair of useless, soft, empty-headed people that would be sure to die of the hunger. Huh!' He spoke very rapidly, and his eyes were fixed on the ground before him. His eyes had a wild, eager light in them as if some primeval impulse were burning within his brain and driving out every other desire but that of asserting his manhood and of subjugating the earth.

'Oh, what do we care who is looking?' said Mary; but she drew back at the same time and gazed distantly at the ground. Then Martin cut the sod, and pressing the spade deep into the earth with his foot, he turned up the first sod with a crunching sound as the grass roots were dragged out of the earth. Mary sighed and walked back hurriedly to her seeds with furrowed brows. She picked up her seeds and began to spread them rapidly to drive out the sudden terror that had seized her at that moment when the first sod was turned up and she saw the fierce, hard look in her husband's eyes, that were unconscious of her presence. She became suddenly afraid of that pitiless, cruel earth, the peasant's slave master, that would keep her chained to hard work and poverty all her life until she would sink again into its bosom. Her short-lived love was gone. Henceforth she was only her husband's helper to till the earth. And Martin, absolutely without thought, worked furiously, covering the ridge with black earth, his sharp spade gleaming white as he whirled it sideways to beat the sods.

Then as the sun rose the little valley beneath the ivy-covered hills became dotted with white frieze shirts, and everywhere men worked madly without speaking and women spread seeds. There was no heat in the light of the sun, and there was a sharpness in the still thin air that made the men jump on their spade hafts ferociously and beat the sods as if they were living enemies. Birds hopped silently before the spades, with their heads cocked sideways, watching for worms. Made brave by hunger they often dashed under the spades to secure their food.

Then when the sun reached a certain point all the women went back to the village to get dinner for their men, and the men worked on without stopping. Then the women returned, almost running, each carrying a tin can with a flannel tied around it and a little bundle tied with a white cloth. Martin threw down his spade when Mary arrived back in the field. Smiling at one another they sat under the hill for their meal. It was the same as their breakfast, tea and bread and butter.

'Ah', said Martin, when he had taken a long draught of tea from his mug, 'is there anything in this world as fine as eating dinner out in the open like this after doing a good morning's work? There, I have done two ridges and a half. That's more than any man in the village could do. Ha!' And he looked at his wife proudly.

'Yes, isn't it lovely', said Mary, looking at the black ridges wistfully. She was just munching her bread and butter. The hurried trip to the village and the trouble of getting the tea ready had robbed her of her appetite. She had to keep blowing at the turf fire with the rim of her skirt, and the smoke nearly blinded her. But now sitting on that grassy knoll, with the valley all round glistening with fresh seaweed and a light smoke rising from the freshly turned earth, a strange joy swept over her. It overpowered that other feeling of dread that had been with her during the morning.

Martin ate heartily, revelling in his great thirst and his great hunger, with every pore of his body open to the pure air. And he looked around at his neighbours' fields boastfully, comparing them with his own. Then he looked at his wife's little round black head and felt very proud of having her as his own. He leaned back on his elbow and took her hand in his. Shyly and in silence, not knowing what to say and ashamed of their gentle feelings, for peasants are always ashamed of feeling refined, they finished eating and still sat hand in hand looking away into the distance. Everywhere the sowers were resting on little knolls, men, women and children sitting in silence. And the great calm of nature in spring filled the atmosphere around them. Everything seemed to sit still and wait until midday had passed. Only the gleaming sun chased westwards at a mighty pace, in and out through white clouds.

Then in a distant field an old man got up, took his spade and began to clean the earth from it with a piece of stone. The rasping noise carried a long way in the silence. That was the signal for a general rising all along the little valley. Young men stretched themselves and yawned. They walked slowly back to their ridges.

Martin's back and his wrists were getting a little sore, and Mary felt that if she stooped again over her seeds that her neck would break, but neither said anything and soon they had forgotten their tiredness in the mechanical movement of their bodies. The strong smell of the upturned earth acted like a drug on their nerves.

In the afternoon, when the sun was strongest, the old men of the village came out to look at their people sowing. Martin's grandfather, almost bent double over his thick stick, stopped in the land outside the field and, groaning loudly, he leaned over the fence.

'God bless the work', he called wheezily.

'And you, grandfather', replied the couple together, but they did not stop working.

'Ha!' muttered the old man to himself. 'Ha! He sows well and that woman is good, too. They are beginning well.'

It was fifty years since he had begun with his Mary, full of hope and pride, and the merciless soil had hugged them to its bosom ever since, each spring without rest. But he did not think of that. The soil gives forgetfulness. Only the present is re-membered in the spring, even by the aged who have spent their lives tilling the earth; so the old man, with his huge red nose and the spotted handkerchief tied around his skull under his black soft felt hat, watched his grandson work and gave him advice.

'Don't cut your sods so long', he would wheeze, 'you are putting too much soil on your ridge.'

'Ah, woman! Don't plant a seed so near the edge. The stalk will come out sideways.'

And they paid no heed to him.

'Ah', grumbled the old man, 'in my young days, when men worked from morning till night without tasting food, better work was done. But of course it can't be expected to be the same as it was. The breed is getting weaker. So it is.'

Then he began to cough in his chest and hobbled away to another field where his son Michael was working.

By sundown Martin had five ridges finished. He threw down his spade and stretched himself. All his bones ached and he wanted to lie down and rest. 'It's time to be going home, Mary,' he said.

Mary straightened herself, but she was too tired to reply. She looked at Martin wearily and it seemed to her that it was a great many years since they had set out that morning. Then she thought of the journey home and the trouble of feeding the pigs, putting the fowls into their coops and getting the supper ready and a momentary flash of rebellion against the slavery of being a peasant's wife crossed her mind. It passed in a moment. Martin was saying, as he dressed himself:

'Ha! My soul from the devil, it has been a good day's work.

11

Five ridges done, and each one of them as straight as a steel rod. Begob, Mary it's no boasting to say that ye might well be proud of being the wife of Martin Delaney. And that's not saying the whole of it, my girl. You did your share better than any woman in Inverara could do it this blessed day.'

They stood for a few moments in silence looking at the work they had done. All her dissatisfaction and weariness vanished from Mary's mind with the delicious feeling of comfort that overcame her at having done this work with her husband. They had done it together. They had planted seeds in the earth. The next day and the next and all their lives, when spring came they would have to bend their backs and do it until their hands and bones got twisted with rheumatism. But night would always bring sleep and forgetfulness.

As they walked home slowly Martin walked in front with another peasant talking about the sowing, and Mary walked behind, with her eyes on the ground, thinking.

Cows were lowing at a distance.

THE COW'S DEATH

The calf was still-born. It came from the womb tail first. When its red, unwieldy body dropped on the greensward it was dead. It lay with its head doubled about its neck in a clammy mass. The men stood about it and shook their heads in silence. The wife of the peasant who owned the cow sighed and said, 'It is God's will.' The cow moaned, mad with the pain of birth. Then she wheeled around cumbersomely, her hoofs driving into the soft earth beneath the weight of her body. She stooped over the calf and moaned, again smelling it. Then she licked the still body with her coarse tongue lovingly. The woman rubbed the cow's matted forehead, and there was a tear in her eye; for she too was a mother.

Then the cow, overcome once more with the pain, moved away from the calf and stood with her head bent low, breathing heavily through her nostrils. The breath came in long pale columns, like sunbeams coming through the window of a darkened church. They drove her away to a corner of the field, and she stood wearily with her head over the fence, lashing her flanks with her tail restlessly.

They seized the calf and dragged it by the feet along the field to the fence, out through the fence into another field, then through another fence, then up the grassy slope that led to the edge of the cliff. They dropped it downwards into the sea. It lay in a pulped mass on the rocks. They rebuilt the gaps in the stone fences carefully and returned to the cow. The woman offered her a hot drink of oatmeal, but she refused it. They seized her and poured the drink down her throat, using a bull's horn as a funnel. The cow half swallowed the drink, half tossed it away with her champing mouth.

Then they went home, the woman still moaning the dead calf and apologizing to God for her sorrow. The peasant remained with the cow, watching until she should drop the bag. He buried it under a mound of stones. He dug his heel in the ground, and, taking a handful of the brown earth, he made the sign of the cross on the cow's side. Then he too went home.

For a long time the cow stood leaning over the fence, until the pain lessened. She turned around suddenly and lowed and tossed her head. She took a short run forward, the muscles of her legs creaking like new boots. She stopped again, seeing nothing about her in the field. Then she began to run around by the fence, putting her head over it here and there, lowing. She found nothing. Nothing answered her call. She became wilder as the sense of her loss became clearer to her consciousness. Her eyes became red around the rims and fierce like a bull's. She began to smell around on the ground, half running, half walking, stumbling clumsily among the tummocks of grass.

There was where she had lain in travail, on the side of a little slope, the grass compressed and faded by the weight of her body. There was where she had given birth, the ground trampled by many feet and torn here and there, with the brown earth showing through. Then she smelt where the calf had lain. There were wet stains on the grass. She looked around her fiercely, and then she put her nose to the ground and started to follow the trail where they had dragged the calf to the fence. At the fence she stopped and smelt a long time, wondering with her stupid brain whither the trail led. And then stupidly she pressed with her great bulk against the fence. The stones cut her breast, but she pressed harder in terror and the fence fell before her. She stumbled through the gap and cut her left thigh near the udder. She did not heed the pain, but pressed forward, smelling the trail and snorting.

Faster she went, and now and again she raised her head and lowed – a long, mournful low that ended in a fierce *crescendo*, – like a squall of wind coming around a corner. At the second fence she paused again. Again she pressed against it, and again it fell before her. Going through the gap she got caught, and in the struggle to get through she cut both her sides along the flanks. The blood trickled through jaggedly, discolouring the white streak on the left flank.

She came at a run up the grassy slope to the cliff. She shuddered and jerked aside when she suddenly saw the sea and heard it rumbling distantly below – the waves seething on the rocks and the sea birds calling dismally with their noisome cackle. She smelt the air in wonder. Then she slowly advanced, inch by inch, trembling. When she reached the summit, where the grass ended in a gravel belt that dropped down to the sheer slope of rock, she rushed backwards, and circled around wildly, lowing. Again she came up, and planting her feet carefully on the gravel, she looked down. The trail of her calf ended there. She could follow it no further. It was lost in the emptiness beyond that gravel ledge. She tried to smell the air, but nothing reached her nostrils but the salt smell of the sea. She moaned and her sides heaved with the outrush of her breath. Then she looked down, straining out her neck. She saw the body of her calf on the rocks below.

She uttered a joyful cry and ran backwards, seeking a path to descend. Up and down the summit of the cliff she went, smelling here and there, looking out over the edge, going on her knees and looking down and finding nowhere a path that led to the object on the rocks below. She came back again, her hind legs clashing as she ran, to the point where the body had been dropped over the precipice.

She strained out and tapped with her fore hoof, scratching the gravel and trying to descend, but there was nothing upon which she could place her feet – just a sheer drop of one hundred feet of cliff and her calf lay on the rocks below.

She stood stupidly looking at it a long time, without moving a muscle. Then she lowed, calling to her calf, but no answer came. She saw the water coming in with the tide, circling around the calf on the rocks. She lowed again, warning it. Wave after wave came in, eddying around the body. She lowed again and tossed her head wildly as if she wanted to buffet the waves with her horns.

And then a great wave came towering in, and catching up the calf on its crest swept it from the rocks.

And the cow, uttering a loud bellow, jumped headlong down.

THE WAVE

The cliff was two hundred feet high. It sloped outwards from its grassy summit, along ten feet of brown gravel, down one hundred and seventy feet of grey limestone, giant slabs piled horizontally with large slits between the slabs where sea-birds nested. The outward slope came to a round point twenty feet from the base and there the cliff sank inwards, making a dark cavern along the cliff's face into the bowels of the earth. At the mouth the cavern was twenty feet high and at the rear its roof touched its floor, a flat rock that stretched from the base of the cliff to the sea. The cavern had a black-slate roof and at the rear there was a large streak of yellow gravel.

The cliff was semicircular. And at each corner a black jagged reef jutted from its base out into the sea. Between the reefs there was a little cove. But the sea did not reach to the semicircle of the cliff. Only its waves swept up from the deep over the flat rock to the cliff. The sea had eaten up the part of the cliff that rested on that semicircle of flat rock, during thousands of years of battle.

It was nearly high tide. But the sea moved so violently that the two reefs bared with each receding wave until they seemed to be long shafts of black steel sunk into the bowels of the ocean. Their thick manes of red seaweed were sucked stiff by each fleeing wave. The waves came towering into the cove across both reefs, confusedly, meeting midway in the cove, chasing one another, climbing over one another's backs, spitting savage columns of green and white water vertically, when their arched manes clashed. In one monstrous stride they crossed the flat rock. Then with a yawning sound they swelled up mid-way in the cliff. There was a mighty roar as they struck the cliff and rebounded. Then they sank again, dishevelled masses of green and white, hurrying backward. They rose and fell from the bosom of the ocean, like the heavy breathing of a gluttonous giant.

Then the tide reached its highest point and there was a pause. The waves hardly made any noise as they struck the cliff, and they drivelled backwards slowly. The trough of the sea between the reefs was convulsing like water in a shaken glass. The cliff's face was black, drenched with brine, that streamed from its base, each tiny rivulet noisy in the sudden silence.

Then the silence broke. The sea rushed back. With the speed and motion of a bladder bursting it sprang backwards. Then it rose upwards in a concave wall, from reef to reef, across the cove, along whose bottom the slimy weeds of the ocean depths were visible through the thin sheet of water left to cover the sea's nakedness by the fury of the rising wave.

For a moment the wave stood motionless, beautifully wild and immense. Its base in front was ragged, uneven and scratched with white foam, like the debris strewn around a just-constructed pyramid. Then a belt of dark blue ran from end to end across its face, sinking inwards in a perfect curve. Then came a wider belt, a green belt peppered with white spots. Then the wave's head curved outwards, arched like the neck of an angry swan. That curved head was a fathom deep, of a transparent green, with a rim of milky white. And to the rear, great lumps of water buttressed it, thousands of tons of water in each lump.

The wave advanced, slowly at first, with a rumbling sound. That awful mass of water advanced simultaneously from end to end of its length without breaking a ripple on its ice-smooth breast. But from its summit a shower of driven foam arose, from east to west, and fell backwards on to the shoulders of the sea that came behind the wave in mountains pushing it to the cliff. The giant cliff looked small in front of that moving wall of blue and green and white water.

Then there was a roar. The wave sprang upwards to its full height. Its crest broke and points of water stuck out, curving downwards like fangs. It seemed to bend its head as it hurtled forward to ram the cliff. In a moment the wave and the cliff had disappeared in a tumbling mass of white water that yawned and hissed and roared. The whole semi-circle of the cliff vanished in the white water and the foam mist that rose above it blotting out the sky. Just for one moment it was thus. In another moment the broken wave had fallen, flying to the sea in a thousand rushing fragments. The cliff appeared again.

But a great black mouth had opened in its face, at the centre, above the cavern. The cliff's face stood ajar, as if it yawned, tired of battle. The mouth was vertical in the cliff, like a ten-foot wedge stuck upwards from the edge of the cavern. Then the cliff tried to close the mouth. It pressed in on it from either side. But it did not close. The sides fell inwards and the mouth grew wider. The whole centre of the cliff broke loose at the top and

17

swayed forward like a tree being felled. There was a noise like rising thunder. Black dust rose from the tottering cliff through the falling foam of the wave. Then with a soft splash the whole centre of the cliff collapsed into the cavern. The sides caved in with another splash. A wall of grey dust arose shutting out everything. The rumbling of moving rocks came through the cloud of dust. Then the cloud rose and went inland.

The cliff had disappeared. The land sloped down to the edge of the cove. Huge rocks stood awkwardly on the very brink of the flat rock, with the rim of the sea playing between them. Smoke was rising from the fallen cliff. And the wave had disappeared. Already another one was gathering in the cove.

THE TRAMP

There were eight paupers in the convalescent yard of the work-house hospital. The yard was an oblong patch of cement with the dining-room on one side and a high red-brick wall on the other. At one end was the urinal and at the other a little tarred wooden shed where there was a bathroom and a wash-house. It was very cold, for the sun had not yet risen over the buildings that crowded out the yard almost from the sky. It was a raw bleak February morning, about eight o'clock.

The paupers had just come out from breakfast and stood about uncertain what to do. What they had eaten only made them hungry and they stood shivering, making muffs of their coat sleeves, their little black woollen caps perched on their heads, some still chewing a last mouthful of bread, others scowling savagely at the ground as they conjured up memories of hearty meals eaten some time in the past.

As usual Michael Deignan and John Finnerty slouched off into the wash-house and leaned against the sink, while they banged their boots on the floor to keep warm. Deignan was very tall and lean. He had a pale melancholy face and there was something the matter with the iris of his right eye. It was not blue like the other eye, but of an uncertain yellowish colour that made one think, somehow, that he was a sly, cunning, deceitful fellow, a totally wrong impression. His hair was very grey around the temples and fair elsewhere. The fingers of his hands were ever so long and thin and he was always chewing at the nails and looking at the ground, wrapped in thought.

'It's very cold', he said in a thin, weak, listless voice. It was almost inaudible.

'Yes', replied Finnerty gruffly, as he started up and heaved a loud sigh. 'Ah—' he began and then he stopped, snorted twice to clear his nose, and let his head fall on his chest. He was a middle-sized, thick-set fellow, still in good condition and fat in the face, which was round and rosy, with grey eyes and very white teeth. His black hair was grown long and curled about his ears. His hands were round, soft and white, like a school-master's.

The two of them stood leaning their backs against the wash-stand and stamped their feet in a moody silence for several minutes and then the tramp who had been admitted to the hospital the previous night wandered into the wash-house. He appeared silently at the entrance of the shed and paused there for a moment while his tiny blue eyes darted around piercingly yet softly, just like a graceful wild animal might look through a clump of trees in a forest. His squat low body, standing between the tarred doorposts of the shed with the concrete wall behind and the grey sky overhead, was after a fashion menacing with the power and vitality it seemed to exude. So it seemed at least to the two dejected, listless paupers within the shed. They looked at the tramp with a mournful vexed expression and an envious gleam in their eyes and a furrowing of their foreheads and a shrinking of their flesh from this fresh dominant coarse lump of aggressive wandering life, so different to their own jaded, terror-stricken lives. Each thought, 'Look at the red fat face of that vile tramp. Look at his fierce insulting eyes, that stare you in the face as boldly as a lion, or a child, and are impudent enough to have a gentle expression at the back of them, unconscious of malice. Look at that huge black beard that covers all his face and neck except the eyes and the nose and a narrow red slit for the mouth. My God, what throat muscles and what hair on his chest, on a day like this too, when I would die of cold to expose my chest that way!'

So each thought and neither spoke. As the tramp grinned foolishly – he just opened his beard, exposed red lips and red gums with stray blackened teeth scattered about them and then closed the beard again – the two paupers made no response. The two of them were educated men, and without meaning it they shrank from associating with the unseemly dirty tramp on terms of equality, just as they spent the day in the wash-house in the cold, so as to keep away from the other paupers.

The tramp took no further notice of them. He went to the back of the shed and stood there looking out of the door and chewing tobacco. The other two men, conscious of his presence and irritated by it, fidgeted about and scowled. At last the tramp looked at Deignan, grinned, fumbled in his coat pocket, took out a crumpled cigarette and handed it to Deignan with another grin and a nodding of his head. But he did not speak.

Deignan had not smoked a cigarette for a week. As he looked at it for a moment in wonder, his bowels ached with desire for the little thin, crumpled, dirt-stained roll of tobacco held between the thumb and forefinger of the tramp's gnarled and mud-caked hand. Then with a contortion of his face as he tried to swallow his breath he muttered, 'You're a brick', and stretched out a trembling hand. In three seconds the cigarette was lit and he was inhaling the first delicious puff of drug-laden smoke. His face lit up with a kind of delicious happiness. His eyes sparkled. He took three puffs and was handing the cigarette to his friend when the tramp spoke.

'No, keep it yerself, towny', he said in his even effortless soft voice. 'I've got another for him.'

And then when the two paupers were smoking, their listlessness vanished and they became cheerful and talkative. The two cigarettes broke down the barriers of distrust and contempt between themselves and the tramp. His unexpected act of generosity had counteracted his beard and the degraded condition of his clothes. He was not wearing a pauper's uniform, but patched corduroy trousers and numbers of waistcoats and tattered coats of all colours, piled indiscriminately on his body and held together not by buttons but by a cord tied around his waist. They accepted him as a friend. They began to talk to him.

'You just came in for the night?' asked Deignan. There was still a condescending tone in the cultured accents.

The tramp nodded. Then after several seconds he rolled his tobacco to the other cheek, spat on the floor and hitched up his trousers.

'Yes', he said. 'I walked from Drogheda yesterday and I landed in Dublin as tired as a dog. I said to myself that the only place to go was in here. I needed a wash, a good bed and a rest, and I had only ninepence, a piece of steak, a few spuds and an onion. If I bought a bed they'd be all gone and now I've had a good sleep, a warm bath, and I still have my ninepence and my grub. I'll start off soon as I get out at eleven o'clock and maybe walk fifteen miles before I put up for the night somewhere.'

'But how did you get into the hospital ward?' asked Finnerty, eyeing the tramp with a jealous look. The cigarette had accentuated Finnerty's feeling of hunger, and he was irritated at the confident way the tramp talked of walking fifteen miles that day and putting up somewhere afterwards.

'How did I get in?' said the tramp. 'That's easy. I got a rash on my right leg this three years. It always gets me into the hospital when I strike a workhouse. It's easy.'

Again there was a silence. The tramp shuffled to the door and looked out into the yard. The sky overhead was still grey and bleak. The water that had been poured over the concrete yard to wash it two hours before, still glistened in drops and lay in little pools here and there. There was no heat in the air to dry it.

The other six paupers, three old men with sticks, two young

men and a youth whose pale face was covered with pimples, were all going about uncertainly, talking in a tired way and peering greedily in through the windows of the dining-room, where old Neddy, the pauper in charge of the dining-room, was preparing the bread and milk for the dinner ration. The tramp glanced around at all this and then shrugged his shoulders and shuffled back to the end of the wash-house.

'How long have you been in here?' he asked Deignan.

Deignan stubbed the remainder of his cigarette against his boot, put the quenched piece in the lining of his cap and then said, 'I've been here six months.'

'Educated man?' said the tramp. Deignan nodded. The tramp looked at him, went to the door and spat and then came back to his former position:

'I'll say you're a fool', he said quite coolly. 'There doesn't look to be anything the matter with you. In spite of your hair, I bet you're no more than thirty-five. Eh?'

'That's just right about my age, but—'

'Hold on', said the tramp. 'You are as fit as a fiddle, this is a spring morning, and yer loafing in here and eating yer heart out with hunger and misery instead of taking to the roads. What man! You're mad. That's all there's to it.' He made a noise with his tongue as if driving a horse and began to clap his hands on his bare chest. Every time he hit his chest there was a dull heavy sound like distant thunder. The noise was so loud that Deignan could not speak until the tramp stopped beating his chest. He stood wriggling his lips and winking his right eye in irritation against what the tramp had said and jealousy of the man's strength and endurance, beating his bare hairy chest that way on such a perishing day. The blows would crush Deignan's ribs and the exposure would give him pneumonia.

'It's all very well for you to talk', he began querulously. Then he stopped and looked at the tramp. It occurred to him that it would be ridiculous to talk to a tramp about personal matters. But there was something aggressive and dominant and yet absolutely unemotional in the tramp's fierce stare that drove out that feeling of contempt. Instead Deignan felt spurred to defend himself. 'How could you understand me?' he continued. 'As far as you can see I am all right. I have no disease but a slight rash on my back and that comes from underfeeding, from hunger and . . . and depression. My mind is sick. But of course you don't understand that.'

'Quite right,' said Finnerty, blowing cigarette smoke through his nostrils moodily. 'I often envy those who don't think. I wish I were a farm labourer.'

22

'Huh.' The tramp uttered the exclamation in a heavy roar. Then he laughed loudly and deeply, stamped his feet and banged his chest. His black beard shook with laughter. 'Mother of Mercy,' he cried, 'I'll be damned but you make me laugh, the two of you.'

The two shuffled with their feet and coughed and said nothing. They became instantly ashamed of their contemptuous thoughts for the tramp, he who a few minutes before had given them cigarettes. They suddenly realized that they were paupers, degraded people, and contemptible people for feeling superior to a fellow man because he was a tramp. They said nothing. The tramp stopped laughing and became serious.

'Now look here,' he said to Deignan, what were you in civilian life, as they say to soldiers, what did you do before you came in here?'

'Oh the last job I had was a solicitor's clerk', murmured Deignan, biting his nails. 'But that was only a stopgap, I can't say that I ever had anything permanent. Somehow I always seemed to drift. When I left college I tried for the Consular Service and failed. Then I stayed at home for a year at my mother's place in Tyrone. She has a little estate there. Then I came to Dublin here. I got disgusted hanging around at home. I fancied everybody was pitying me. I saw everybody getting married or doing something while I only loafed about, living on my mother. So I left. Landed here with two portmanteaux and eighty-one pounds. It's six years ago next fifteenth of May. A beautiful sunny day it was too'.

Deignan's plaintive voice drifted away into silence and he gnawed his nails and stared at the ground. Finnerty was trying to get a last puff from the end of his cigarette. He was trying to hold the end between his thumbs and puckered up his lips as if he were trying to drink boiling milk. The tramp silently handed him another cigarette and then he turned to Deignan.

'What did ye do with the eighty-one quid?' he said. 'Did ye drink it or give it to the women?'

Finnerty, cheered by the second cigarette which he had just lit, uttered a deep guffaw and said, 'Ha, the women blast them, they're the curse of many a man's life', but Deignan started up and his face paled and his lips twitched.

'I can assure you', he said, 'that I never touched a woman in my life.' He paused as if to clear his mind of the horror that the tramp's suggestion had aroused in him. 'No, I can't say I drank it. I can't say I did anything at all. I just drifted from one job to another. Somehow, it seemed to me that nothing big

23

could come my way and that it didn't matter very much how I spent my life, because I would be a failure anyway. Maybe I did drink too much once in a while, or dropped a few pounds at a race meeting, but nothing of any account. No, I came down just because I seemed naturally to drift downwards and I couldn't muster up courage to stop myself. I...I've been here six months ... I suppose I'll die here.'

'Well I'll be damned', said the tramp. He folded his arms on his chest, and his chest heaved in and out with his excited breathing. He kept looking at Deignan and nodding his head. Finnerty who had heard Deignan's story hundreds of times with numberless details shrugged his shoulders, sniffed and said: 'Begob, it's a funny world. Though I'm damn sure that I wouldn't be here only for women and drink.'

'No?' said the tramp. 'How do you make that out?'

'No by Jiminy', said Finnerty, blowing out a cloud of blue smoke through his mouth as he talked. 'I'd be a rich man to-day only for drink and women.' He crossed his feet and leaned jauntily back against the washstand, with his hands held in front of him, the fingers of the right hand tapping the back of the left. His fat round face, with the heavy jaw, turned sideways towards the doorway, looked selfish, stupid and cruel. He laughed and said in an undertone, 'Oh boys, oh boys, when I come to think of it.' Then he coughed and shrugged his shoulders. 'Would you believe it', he said turning to the tramp, 'I've spent five thousand pounds within the last twelve months? It's a fact. Upon my soul I have. I curse the day I got hold of that money. Until two years ago I was a happy man. I had one of the best schools in the south of Ireland. Then an aunt of mine came home from America and stayed in the house with my mother and myself. She died within six months and left mother five thousand pounds. I got it out of the old woman's hands, God forgive me, and then . . . Oh well', Finnerty shook his head solemnly, raised his eyebrows and sighed. 'I'm not sorry', he continued, leering at a black spot on the concrete floor of the wash-house. 'I could count the number of days I was sober on my fingers and thumbs. And now I'd give a month of my life for a cup of tea and a hunk of bread.' He stamped about clapping his hands and laughing raucously. His bull neck shook when he laughed. Then he scowled again and said, 'Wish I had a penny. That's nine o'clock striking. I'm starving with the hunger.'

'Eh? Hungry?' The tramp had fallen into a kind of doze while Finnerty had been talking. He started up, scratched his bare neck and then rummaged within his upper garments mumbling to himself. At last he drew forth a little bag from which he took three pennies. He handed the pennies to Finnerty. 'Get chuck for the three of us', he said.

Finnerty's eye gleamed, he licked his lower lip with his tongue and then he darted out without saying a word.

In the workhouse hospital a custom had grown up, since goodness knows when, that the pauper in charge of the dining-room was allowed to filch a little from the hospital rations, of tea, bread and soup, and then sell them to the paupers again as extras at nine o'clock in the morning for a penny a portion. This fraudulent practice was overlooked by the ward-master; for he himself filched all his rations from the paupers' hospital supply and he did it with the connivance of the workhouse master, who was himself culpable in other ways and was therefore prevented by fear from checking his subordinates. But Finnerty did not concern himself with these things. He dived into the dining-room, held up the three pennies before old Neddy's face and whispered 'Three.' Neddy, a lean wrinkled old pauper with a very thick red under-lip like a negro, was standing in front of the fire with his hands folded under his dirty check apron. He counted the three pennies, mumbling, and then put them in his pocket. During twenty years he had collected ninety-three pounds in that manner. He had no relatives to whom he could bequeath the money, he never spent any and he never would leave the workhouse until his death, but he kept on collecting the money. It was his only pleasure in life. When he had collected a shilling in pennies he changed it into silver and the silver in due course into banknotes.

'They say he has a hundred pounds', thought Finnerty, his mouth dry with greed, as he watched Neddy put away the pennies. 'Wish I knew where it was. I'd strangle him here and now and make a run for it. A hundred pounds. I'd eat and eat and then I'd drink and drink.'

The tramp and Deignan never spoke a word until Finnerty came back, carrying three bowls of tea and three hunks of bread on a white deal board. Deignan and Finnerty immediately began to gulp their tea and tear at the bread, but the tramp merely took a little sip at the tea and then took up his piece of bread, broke it in two and gave a piece to each of the paupers.

'I'm not hungry', he said. 'I've got my dinner with me, and as soon as I get out along the road in the open country I'm going to sit down and cook it. And it's going to be a real spring day, too. Look at that sun.'

The sun had at last mounted the wall. It was streaming into the yard lighting up everything. It was not yet warm, but it was cheering and invigorating. And the sky had become a clear pure blue colour.

'Doesn't it make ye want to jump and shout', cried the tramp, joyously stamping about. He had become very excited, seeing the sun.

'I'm afraid I'd rather see a good dinner in front of me', muttered Finnerty with his mouth full of bread.

'What about you, towny?' said the tramp, standing in front of Deignan. 'Wouldn't ye like to be walking along a mountain road now with a river flowing under yer feet in a valley and the sun tearing at yer spine?'

Deignan looked out wistfully, smiled for a moment dreamily and then sighed and shook his head. He sipped his tea and said nothing. The tramp went to the back of the shed. Nobody spoke until they had finished the bread and tea. Finnerty collected the bowls.

'I'll take these back', he said, 'and maybe I might get sent over to the cookhouse for something.'

He went away and didn't come back. The tramp and Deignan fell into a contemplative doze. Neither spoke until the clock struck ten. The tramp shrugged himself and coming over to Deignan, tapped him on the arm.

'I was thinking of what you said about . . . about how you spent your life, and I thought to myself, "Well, that poor man is telling the truth and he's a decent fellow, and it's a pity to see him wasting his life in here." That's just what I said to myself. As for that other fellow. He's no good. He's a liar. He'll go back again to his school or maybe somewhere else. But neither you nor I are fit to be respectable citizens. The two of us were born for the road, towny. Only you never had the courage of your convictions.'

The tramp went to the door and spat. Deignan had been looking at him in wonder while he was talking and now he shifted his position restlessly and furrowed his forehead.

'I can't follow you', he said nervously and he opened his mouth to continue, when again he suddenly remembered that the man was a tramp and that it would not be good form to argue with him on matters of moral conduct.

'Of course ye can't', said the tramp, shuffling back to his position. Then he stuck his hands within his sleeves and shifted his tobacco to his other cheek. 'I know why you can't follow me. You're a Catholic, you believe in Jesus Christ and the Blessed Virgin and the priests and a heaven hereafter. You like to be called respectable and to pay your debts. You were born a free man like myself, but you didn't have the courage . . . '

'Look here, man', cried Deignan in a shocked and angry voice, 'stop talking that rubbish. You have been very kind about – er – cigarettes and food, but I can't allow you to blaspheme our holy religion in my presence. Horrid. Ugh.'

The tramp laughed noiselessly, There was silence for several moments. Then the tramp went up to Deignan, shook him fiercely by the right arm and shouted in his ear. 'You're the biggest fool I ever met.' Then he laughed aloud and went back to his place. Deignan began to think that the tramp was mad and grew calm and said nothing.

'Listen here', said the tramp. 'I was born disreputable. My mother was a fisherman's daughter and my lawful father was a farm labourer, but my real father was a nobleman and I knew it when I was ten years old. That's what gave me a disreputable outlook on life. My father gave mother money to educate me, and of course she wanted to make me a priest. I said to myself, I might as well be one thing as another. But at the age of twenty-three when I was within two years of ordination a servant girl had a child and I got expelled. She followed me, but I deserted her after six months. She lost her looks after the birth of the child. I never clapped eyes on her or the child since.' He paused and giggled. Deignan bit his lip and his face contorted with disgust.

'I took to the road then', said the tramp. 'I said to myself that it was a foolish game trying to do anything in this world but sleep and eat and enjoy the sun and the earth and sea and the rain. That was twenty-two years ago. And I'm proud to say that I never did a day's work since and never did a fellow-man any injury. That's my religion and it's a good one. Live like the birds, free. That's the only way for a free man to live. Look at yourself in a looking-glass. I'm ten years older than you and yet you look old enough to be my father. Come, man, take to the road with me to-day. I know you're a decent fellow, so I'll show you the ropes. In six months from now you'll forget you were ever a pauper or a clerk. What d'ye say?'

Deignan mused, looking at the ground.

'Anything would be better than this', he muttered. 'But . . . Good Lord, becoming a tramp! I may have some chance of getting back to respectable life from here, but once I became a tramp I should be lost.'

'Lost? What would you lose?'

Deignan shrugged his shoulders.

'I might get a job. Somebody might discover me here. Some-body might die. Anything might happen. But if I went on the road ... He shrugged his shoulders again.

'So you prefer to remain a pauper?' said the tramp with an impudent, half-contemptuous grin. Deignan winced and he felt a sudden mad longing grow within his head to do something mad and reckless.

'You're a fine fellow', continued the tramp, 'you prefer to rot in idleness here with old men and useless wrecks to coming out into the free air. What man! Pull yerself together and come over now with me and apply for yer discharge. We'll foot it out together down south. What d'ye say?'

'By Jove, I think I will!' cried Deignan with a gleam in his eyes. He began to trot excitedly around the shed, going to the door and looking up at the sky, and coming back again and looking at the ground, fidgeting with his hands and feet. 'D'ye think, would it be all right?' he kept saying to the tramp.

'Sure it will be all right', the tramp kept answering. 'Come on with me to the ward master and ask for your discharge.'

But Deignan would not leave the shed. He had never in all his life been able to come to a decision on an important matter.

'Do you think, would it be all right?' he kept saying.

'Oh damn it and curse it for a story', said the tramp at last, 'stay where you are and good day to you, I'm off.'

He shuffled out of the shed and across the yard. Deignan put out his hand and took a few steps forward.

'I say – ' he began and then stopped again. His brain was in a whirl thinking of green fields, mountain rivers, hills clad in blue mists, larks singing over clover fields, but something made him unable to loosen his legs so that they could run after the tramp.

'I say – ' he began again, and then he stopped and his face shivered and beads of sweat came out on his forehead.

He could not make up his mind.

THE ROCKFISH

Flop. The cone-shaped bar of lead tied to the end of the fishing-line dropped into the sea without causing a ripple. It sank rapidly through the long seaweed that grew on the face of the rock. It sank twenty-five feet and then struck the bottom. It tumbled around and then lay on its side in a niche at the top of a round pool. The man on top of the rock hauled in his line until it was taut. The bar of lead bobbled up and down twice. Then it rested straight on its end in the niche. Three short plaits of stiff horsehair extended crookedly like tentacles from the line above the leaden weight at regular intervals. At the end of each plait was a hook baited all over with shelled periwinkle. A small crab, transfixed through the belly, wriggled on the lowest hook. The two upper hooks had a covering of crushed crab tied by thin strings around the periwinkles. The three baited hooks swung round and round, glistening white through the red strands of broad seaweed that hung lazily from their stems in the rock face. Dark caverns at the base of the rock cast long shadows out over the bottom of the sea about the hooks. Little bulbous things growing in groups on the bottom spluttered methodically as they stirred.

The man sitting above on the top of the rock spat into the sea. Resting his fishing-rod in the crutch of his right arm, he began to fill his pipe, yawning.

A little rockfish came rushing out from a cavern under the rock. He whisked his tail and stopped dead behind a huge blade of seaweed when he saw the glistening baits. His red scaly body was the colour of the weed. It tapered from the middle to the narrow tail and to the triangular-shaped head. He stared at the baits for a long time without moving his body. His gills rose and fell steadily. Then he flapped his tail and glided to the upper hook. He touched it with his snout. He nibbled at it timorously three times. Then he snatched at the top of it and darted away back into the cavern with a piece of periwinkle in his mouth. The man on the rock sat up excitedly, threw his pipe on the rock, and seized the rod with both hands, breathing through his nose.

Several rockfish gathered around the little fellow in the cavern. They tried to snatch the piece of periwinkle from his mouth. But he dived under a ledge of rock and bolted it hurriedly. Then, all the rockfish darted out to the hooks. The little ones scurried around hither and thither. Three middle-sized ones stood by the two upper hooks, sniffing at them. Then they began to nibble carefully. One little rockfish stood on his head over the bottom hook and sniffed at it. But the crab wriggled one leg and the rockfish darted away at a terrific speed. All the rockfish darted away after it into the cavern. Then one of the middle-sized ones came back again alone. He went up to the highest hook and grabbed at it immediately. He took the whole bait from it. The hook grazed his lower lip as it slipped from his mouth. The rockfish dropped the bait, turned a somersault, and dived into the cavern.

The man on the rock swung his rod back over his head, and dropped it forward again with an oath when he found the line coming slack. 'Missed', he said. Then the leaden weight slipped back again into the niche. A crowd of rockfish quarrelled over the pieces of periwinkle fallen from the middle-sized fellow's mouth. The pieces, too light to sink, kept floating about. Then they disappeared one by one into the fishes' mouths.

A huge rockfish prowled in from the deep. He stood by the corner of a rock watching the little ones quarrel over the pieces of fallen bait. He was as big as all the others together. He must have been three feet long and his middle was as thick as a bull-dog's chest. The scales on his back were all the colours of the rainbow. His belly was a dun colour. He stood still for a time, watching like an old bull, his gills showing large red cavities in his throat as they opened. Then he swooped in among the little ones. They dived away from him into the cavern. He gobbled the remaining pieces of bait. Then he turned around slowly twice and swam close to the bottom towards the hooks. He saw the crab wriggling on the lowest hook. With a rush he swallowed the crab and the hook, turned about and rushed away with it, out towards his lair in the deep. The leaden weight rushed along the bottom with him. The line went taut with a snap over his back. The fishing-rod was almost wrenched from the hands of the man on the rock. Its tip touched the water. Then the man heaved the rod over his head and grasped the line. The hook was wrenched back out of the rockfish's gullet and its point tore through the side of his mouth.

The rockfish was whirled about by the wrench and dragged backwards headlong. With a swishing sound he heaved straight through the water towards the cavern. Then the line went taut again as the man hauled in. The rockfish was tugged up along the face of the rock. He jumped twice and heaved. He tore a strip of the soft thick skin in which the hook was embedded from his jaw at one end. Hanging to the hook by this strip, he came up gasping through the hanging weeds. The man groaned as he heaved.

Then the bared top hook got caught in a broad blade of seaweed. It combed its way through to the hard stem and then got stuck. The man heaved and could draw it no farther. The rockfish hung exhausted from the bottom hook. The man stuck his right foot against a ledge and leaning back with the line held in his two hands across his stomach he pulled with all his might. The top hook broke. The line jerked up. The rockfish reached the surface. He tried to breathe with wide open mouth. Then he hurled himself into the air and dived headlong downwards. The hanging strip of skin parted from his jaw. He was free.

THE LANDING

Two old women were sitting on the rocks that lay in a great uneven wall along the seashore beyond the village of Rundangan. They were knitting. Their red petticoats formed the only patch of colour among the grey crags about them and behind them. In front of them stretched the sea, blue and calm. It sparkled far out where the sun was shining on it. The sky was blue and empty and the winds were silent. The only noise came from the sea, near the shore, where it was just low tide. The water babbled and flopped along the seaweed on the low rocks that lay afar out, black strips of rocks with red seaweed growing on them. It was a spring evening and the air was warm and fresh, as if it had just been sprinkled with eau de cologne or something. The old women were talking in low voices sleepily as they knitted woollen stockings. 'Ah yes', said one of them called Big Bridget Conlon, an old woman of seventy, a woman of great size and strength, with big square jaws like a man, high cheekbones, red complexion and wistful blue eyes that always seemed to be in mourning about something. She made a wedge of a corner of the little black shawl that was tied around her neck and cleaned out her right ear with it. 'I don't know', she said, 'why it is, but I always get a pain in that ear when there's bad weather coming. There it is now, just as if there was a little stream running along inside in it. My grandmother, God have mercy on her, suffered the same way.'

'Yes', said the other woman, with a lazy and insincere sigh, 'there is no going against tokens that are sent that way.' The other woman, Mary Mullen, was only sixty-five and her reddish hair had not yet turned very grey. She had shifty grey eyes and she was very thin about the body. She was greatly feared in the fishing village of Rundangan for her slandering tongue, and her habit of listening by night at other people's doors to eavesdrop on their conversation.

'Heh, heh', said Big Bridget, looking out mournfully at the sea, 'sure, we only live by the Grace of God, sure enough, with the sea always watching to devour us. And yet only for it we would starve. Sure, many a thing is a queer thing, sure enough.' She stuck the end of a knitting needle against her teeth and leaned her head against it. With brooding eyes she looked out at the sea that way, as if she were trying to explain something to herself.

The two old women lapsed into silence again and knitted away. The tide turned and it began to flow. From where the women sat the land stretched out on either side into the sea. To the east of them, it stretched out in high cliffs, and to the west it ran along almost level with the sea for about a mile, a bare stretch of naked grey rock strewn with boulders. Farther west it rose gradually into high cliffs. Now a light breeze crept along the crags in fitful gusts, here and there, irregularly. The women did not notice it.

Then suddenly a sharp gust of wind came up from the sea and blew the old women's petticoats in the air like balloons. It fluttered about viciously for a few moments and then disappeared again. The old women sniffed anxiously and rolled up their knitting by a common impulse before they spoke a word. They looked at one another with furrowed brows.

'What did I say to you, Mary?' said Big Bridget in an awed whisper, in which however there was a weird melancholy note of intense pleasure. She covered her mouth with the palm of her right hand and then made a motion as if she were throwing her teeth at the other woman. It was a customary gesture with her. 'That pain in my ear is always right', she continued; 'it's a storm sure enough.' 'God between us and all harm', said Mary Mullen, 'and that man of mine is out fishing with my son Patrick and Stephen Halloran. Good mother of mercy,' she whimpered uneasily as she got to her feet, 'they are the only people out fishing from the whole village and a storm is coming. Amn't I the unfortunate woman. Drowned, drowned they will be.' Suddenly she worked herself into a wild frenzy of fear and lamentation and she spread her hands out towards the sea. Standing on the summit of the line of boulders with her hands stretched out and wisps of her grey hair flying about her face, while the rising and whistling wind blew her red petticoat backwards so that her lean thighs were sharply outlined, she began to curse the sea and bemoan her fate.

'Oh, God forgive you, woman of no sense', cried Big Bridget, struggling to her feet with difficulty on account of the rheumatic pains she had in her right hip; 'what is this you are saying? Abandoned woman, don't tempt the sea with your words. Don't talk of drowning.' There was a sudden ferocity in her words that was strangely akin to the rapid charges of the wind coming up from the sea about them, cold, contemptuous and biting, like bullets flying across a battlefield fired by unknown men against others whom they have never met, the fierce and destructive movement of maddened nature, blind, and rejoicing in madness. And Mary Mullen, with her hands outstretched, paid no heed to Big Bridget, but shrieked at the top of her voice 'Drowned, drowned they will be.' She also seemed to be possessed with a frenzy in which sorrow and joy had lost their values and had intermingled in some emotion that transcended themselves. The sea began to swell and break its back with rivulets of foam.

People came running down to the beach from the village as the storm grew in intensity. They gathered together on the wall of boulders with the two old women. Soon there was a cluster of red petticoats and heads hooded in little black shawls, while the men stood about talking anxiously and looking out to sea towards the west. The sea was getting rougher with every wave that broke along the rocky beach. It began to growl and toss about and make noises as if monstrous teeth were being ground. It became alive and spoke with a multitude of different yells that inspired the listeners with horror and hypnotized them into feeling mad with the sea. Their faces set in a deep frown and their eyes had a distant fiery look in them. They shouted when they spoke to one another. Each contradicted the other. They swore angrily. They strutted about on the boulders with their hands behind their backs, looking at the sea suspiciously as if they thought it was going to rush up each minute and devour them.

Stephen Halloran's wife squatted down on a boulder beside Mary Mullen, and the two women, whose men were out fishing, became the centre of interest. They arrogated to themselves a vast importance from the fact that their men were in danger of death from a common enemy, the sea. Their faces were lengthened with an expression of sorrow, but there was a fierce pride in their sharp eyes that looked out at the sea with hatred, like the wives of ancient warriors who watched on the ramparts of stone forts while their men fought in front with stone battle-axes against the enemy. Stephen Halloran's wife, a weak featured, pale faced woman with weak eyes that were devoid of eyelashes and were red around the rims, kept rolling her little head from side to side, as she searched the sea to the west, looking out from under her eyebrows and from under the little black shawl that covered her head.

'Ah yes', she was saying, as she rocked her head, 'I told him this morning when he was setting his hooks in order, not to attempt going out, on account of the day that was in it, because it was this day twenty year ago, if anybody remembers it, that my grandfather died of pneumonia.'

34

'Drowned, drowned they will be', shrieked Mary Mullen. She had gone on her two knees on a boulder and she had put on a man's frieze waistcoat. She looked like a diver in it, the way it was buttoned up around her neck and three sizes too big for her.

The crashing of the waves against the cliffs to the east was drowning the wind. The wind came steadily, like the rushing of a great cataract heard at a great distance, but the noises of the sea were continually changing, rising and falling, with the stupendous modulations of an orchestra played by giants. Each sound boomed or hissed or crashed with a horrid distinctness. It stood apart from the other sounds that followed and preceded it as menacing and overwhelming as the visions that crowd on a disordered mind, each standing apart from the others in crazy independence.

Then the curragh with the three men rowing in it hove into sight from the west. A cliff jutted out into the sea, forming a breakwater where its sharp wedge-shaped face ended. Around that cliff the curragh appeared, a tiny black dot on the blue and white sea. For a moment the people saw it and they murmured in an awed loud whisper: 'There they are.' Then the curragh disappeared. It seemed to those on the beach that a monstrous wave surmounted it callously and that it had been engulfed and lost for ever, swallowed into the belly of the ocean. The women shrieked and threw their hands across their breasts and some said, 'Oh Blessed Virgin, succour us.' But the men simply said to one another, 'That was the "Wave of the Reaping Hook" that came down on them.' Still the men had their mouths open and they held their breaths and their bodies leaned forward from the hips watching for the curragh to appear again. It did appear and there was an excited murmur 'Hah, God with them.'

From the promontory where the curragh had just passed there was a lull in the water for a long way and the people could see the curragh coming along it all the time without losing sight of it. They could see the men rowing in it. They said, 'That's Stephen Halloran in the stern. It's a mistake to have him in the stern. He's too weak on his oars for a rough day.' They began to move cautiously down to the brink of the sea, where the curragh would have to effect a landing. As the moment when the curragh would have to risk the landing and the black rocks, on which the three men might be dashed to pieces by the ferocious sea, came near, the men on the beach grew more excited and some shivered. The women began to wail. A great babble of voices rose from the beach, harsh and confused, like

35

the voices of demented people. All gave advice and none took heed of the advice given.

The place where the curragh would have to effect a landing was in the middle of the little cove. It was a jagged rock with a smooth space at the brink of the left-hand corner, where a slab had been cut out of it by a thunderclap a few years before. In calm weather the sea just reached level with the rock at half tide and it was easy to land a curragh there. But now the waves were coming over it like hills that had been overturned and were being rolled along a level plain speedily. The men on the beach stood at the edge of the rock and the line of boulders, fifty yards away from the edge of the sea. Yet the waves were coming to their feet when the sea swelled up. They shook their heads and looked at one another.

Peter Mullen's brother, a lanky man with a lame leg, made a megaphone of his hands and shouted to the men in the curragh, 'Keep away as long as ye can, ye can't come through this sea', but he couldn't be heard ten yards away on account of the noise of the sea and of the wind. The curragh approached until it was within two hundred yards of the landing-place. The people on the beach could see the faces of the rowers distinctly. Their faces were distorted and wild. Their bodies were taut with fear and they moved jerkily with their oars, they legs stiff against the sides of the boat, their teeth bared. Two hundred yards away they turned their boat suddenly sideways and began to row away from the landing-place. Silence fell on those on the beach. The men looked eagerly out at the boat. The women rose to their feet and clasped one another. For half a minute there was silence that way while the men in the boat manoeuvred for position.

Then simultaneously a cry arose from the men on the beach and from the men in the boat. With a singing sound of oars grating against the polished wet wood of the gunwale the curragh swung around to the landing. The singing sound of the oars and the ferocious snapping of the men's breath as they pulled could be heard over the roar of the sea, it came so suddenly. The boat swung in towards the rocks. In a few moments the rowers would be smashed to pieces or in safety.

Then the women standing on the boulders became mad with excitement. They did not shrink in fear from looking at the snaky black canvas coated boat, with three men in her, that was cutting the blue and white water, dashing in on the rocks. They screamed and there was a wild, mad joy in their screams. Big Bridget's eyes were no longer mournful. They were fiery like a man's. All the women except Mary Mullen and Stephen

36

Halloran's wife looked greedily at the curragh, but at the same time they tore their hair and screamed with pretended fear. Mary Mullen fell on her face on the boulder and resting her chin on her hands, she kept biting her little finger and saying in a whisper to herself, 'Oh noble son of my womb.' Stephen Halloran's wife rolled herself in her shawl low down between two boulders and went into hysterics.

And the men in the rapidly advancing boat yelled too, a mad joyous yell, as if the rapidity of their movement, the roaring of the sea, the hypnotic power of the green and white water about them and the wind overhead screaming had driven out fear. In the moment of delirium when their boat bore down on death they no longer feared death.

The boat, the crew, the men on the beach, the women on the boulder were all mingled together for a wild moment in a common contempt of danger. For a moment their cries surmounted the sound of the wind and sea. It was the defiance of humanity hurled in the face of merciless nature. And then again there was a strained pause. The noise of voices vanished suddenly and silence came.

On the back of a wave the boat came riding in, the oars stretched out, their points tipping the water. Then the oars dipped. There was a creak, a splash, a rushing sound, a panting of frightened breath, a hurried mumble of excited voices rose from the men on the beach. The men on the beach waited in two lines with clasped hands. The foremost men were up to their waist in water. The boat rushed in between the two lines. They seized the boat. The wave passed over their heads. There was a wild shriek and then confusion. The boat and the foremost men were covered by the wave. Then the wave receded. The boat and the crew and the men holding the boat were left on the rock, clinging to the rock and to one another, like a dragged dog clings to the earth.

They rushed up the rock with the boat. They had landed safely.

THE BLACKBIRD

He was standing on the top of a stone fence singing as loud as he could. He was trying to drown the harsh babble of the sparrows that were perched in the ivy that grew on the face of the tiny cliff behind him. On three sides the tiny cliff encircled him, making a green sloping grassy valley about him and in front of him. Beyond the valley stretched a wide plain.

With his beak in the air and his throat swelling with sound he poured out his voice over the valley. The shrill chirping of the sparrows grated on his ears as it came from behind him in a confused babble. But he rejoiced, for his own delicious warble re-echoed again and again, high above every other sound in the valley. When the echo of his voice came back to him, with its loudness silvered into an enchanting softness by the creviced cliffs, he became so drunk with pride that he swayed on his slender legs and made his wing feathers flutter. He shut his eyes and bent forward his beak again and again to sing with greater strength. It seemed to him that his throat would melt.

The sun had set. The blue twilight was darkening in the valley. It was time for him to be asleep. But he sang on, drunk with pride. So intent was he on his song that he never noticed the sudden silence that fell on all the birds that had been singing, chirping and twittering behind him. Silence came suddenly except for the nervous questioning, protracted whisper of a robin that hopped from stone to stone in the little rocky field beneath the cliff, thrusting out his breast defiantly with each hop. The ivy on the cliff face had been a moment ago alive with sound, and the ivy leaves had been shaking and fluttering as birds rushed hither and thither through them. Now the ivy was still. Not a bird moved. But the blackbird standing on the fence sang on.

A cat had entered the valley. He came over the brow of the little cliff, scrambled noiselessly down a crevice that was covered with moss and trotted swiftly along under the cliff until the birds stopped singing and chirping. As soon as their voices stopped the cat halted. He stopped dead with his right fore paw raised, his long black body half hidden in a hummock of grass he was passing through, his big eyes already gleaming in the half darkness. Then he began slowly to tip the grass around him

with his snout as if he were going to eat it. He curled his tail up
under him. He lay down slowly on his stomach, just for one
moment, and then with a fierce flashing of his eyes, he took a
short rush forward close to the earth. He saw the blackbird
singing on the fence that stretched across his path in front. The
rush brought him as far as the fence where it ended in the cliff.
Carefully planting paw after paw on the stones, and shaking
each paw as he raised it to climb farther, he mounted the fence
until he reached the top with his head. His large round
whiskered head appeared over the top of the fence and began to
roll around with an awful slowness. Again his eyes reached the
blackbird singing on his right, ten yards in front of him. His
eyes blinked and he made a little bored movement with his head
from side to side as if he were heaving a sigh. He licked his paw.
Then with a sudden and amazing spring he drew his body
noiselessly to the top of the fence and rushed along it for five
yards with his tail outstretched, his eyes blazing with an intense
ferocity. The robin set up a piercing cry. The cat stopped dead.

The blackbird, conscious of the silence behind him, was full
of vanity. He thought that he had overcome the sparrows and
that they were listening in rapturous silence to his delicious
warbling. He heard the robin shriek and he thought that the
warning shriek was a cry of jealous rage. He shook himself and
let all the feathers on his dun body sway with the light breeze
that came up from the valley across his round breast. Then
pushing his head backwards until his neck was almost joined
with his back he broke out into another peal. The cat began to
smell the little patch of blackened moss that grew on a stone in
front of him on the fence.

Then there was silence for several moments. The robin had
suddenly taken fright and flew southwards into the darkness
that seemed to hang in the distance. The blackbird was listening
to the answering call of his own voice coming back to him. The
cat crouched down very low with his head moving from side to
side in an apologetic manner, the light breeze making little
whitish ridges through the dark fur on his back. Then he moved
forward again.

He moved forward just as the blackbird broke once more
into song. His long black body, moving sinuously along the
pointed grey stones, looked ghoulish. The rippling notes
coming from the blackbird's full throat rose in a wild peal of
joy as the cat stole nearer inch by inch until at last he was
within striking distance. He measured the round dun body of
the blackbird with his eyes, and he raised his right fore paw
carefully to thrust it forward to a little round stone whence he

39

intended to spring. His body shivered and then it stretched out. The right forepaw landed on the round stone and . . .

Just then a gust of wind struck the blackbird sideways and made him shiver. It was the first gust of the night wind. It filled him with cold and with the sudden realization that he was making a fool of himself singing out there in complete darkness when all the other birds were gone to bed. Suddenly he thought that the silence was on account of the darkness having fallen and not on account of his wonderful music. He was filled with disgust and, uttering three loud peals of bravado, he rose from the fence just as the cat plunged forward to grasp him. A claw landed in his tail and three little feathers fluttered behind as he flew away, his heart panting with fright, afraid to look behind him.

Behind him the cat lay at the foot of the fence, where he had fallen after his fruitless plunge. His head was turned sideways, he was half fallen on his haunches and he was growling savagely. The sparrows began to twitter in the ivy.

HIS FIRST FLIGHT

The young seagull was alone on his ledge. His two brothers and his sister had already flown away the day before. He had been afraid to fly with them. Somehow when he had taken a little run forward to the brink of the ledge and attempted to flap his wings he became afraid. The great expanse of sea stretched down beneath, and it was such a long way down – miles down. He felt certain that his wings would never support him, so he bent his head and ran away back to the little hole under the ledge where he slept at night. Even when each of his brothers and his little sister, whose wings were far shorter than his own, ran to the brink, flapped their wings, and flew away he failed to muster up courage to take that plunge which appeared to him so desperate. His father and mother had come around calling to him shrilly, upbraiding him, threatening to let him starve on his ledge unless he flew away. But for the life of him he could not move.

That was twenty-four hours ago. Since then nobody had come near him. The day before, all day long, he had watched his parents flying about with his brothers and sister, perfecting them in the art of flight, teaching them how to skim the waves and how to dive for fish. He had, in fact, seen his older brother catch his first herring and devour it, standing on a rock, while his parents circled around raising a proud cackle. And all the morning the whole family had walked about on the big plateau midway down the opposite cliff, taunting him with his cowardice.

The sun was now ascending the sky, blazing warmly on his ledge that faced the south. He felt the heat because he had not eaten since the previous nightfall. Then he had found a dried piece of mackerel's tail at the far end of his ledge. Now there was not a single scrap of food left. He had searched every inch, rooting among the rough, dirt-caked straw nest where he and his brothers and sister had been hatched. He even gnawed at the dried pieces of spotted eggshell. It was like eating part of himself. He had then trotted back and forth from one end of the ledge to the other, his grey body the colour of the cliff, his long grey legs stepping daintily, trying to find some means of reaching his parents without having to fly. But on each side of him the ledge ended in a sheer fall of precipice, with the sea beneath. And between him and his parents there was a deep, wide chasm. Surely he could reach them without flying if he could only move northwards along the cliff face? But then on what could he walk? There was no ledge, and he was not a fly. And above him he could see nothing. The precipice was sheer, and the top of it was perhaps farther away than the sea beneath him.

He stepped slowly out to the brink of the ledge, and, standing on one leg with the other leg hidden under his wing, he closed one eye, then the other, and pretended to be falling asleep. Still they took no notice of him. He saw his two brothers and his sister lying on the plateau dozing, with their heads sunk into their necks. His father was preening the feathers on his white back. Only his mother was looking at him. She was standing on a little high hump on the plateau, her white breast thrust forward. Now and again she tore at a piece of fish that lay at her feet, and then scraped each side of her beak on the rock. The sight of the food maddened him. How he loved to tear food that way, scraping his beak now and again to whet it! He uttered a low cackle. His mother cackled too, and looked over at him.

'Ga, ga, ga', he cried, begging her to bring him over some food. 'Gaw-ool-ah', she screamed back derisively. But he kept calling plaintively, and after a minute or so he uttered a joyful scream. His mother had picked up a piece of fish and was flying across to him with it. He leaned out eagerly, tapping the rock with his feet, trying to get nearer to her as she flew across. But when she was just opposite to him, abreast of the ledge, she halted, her legs hanging limp, her wings motionless, the piece of fish in her beak almost within reach of his beak. He waited a moment in surprise, wondering why she did not come nearer, and then, maddened by hunger, he dived at the fish. With a loud scream he fell outwards and downwards into space. His mother had swooped upwards. As he passed beneath her he heard the swish of her wings. Then a monstrous terror seized him and his heart stood still. He could hear nothing. But it only lasted a moment. The next moment he felt his wings spread outwards. The wind rushed against his breast feathers, then under his stomach and against his wings. He could feel the tips of his wings cutting through the air. He was not falling head-long now. He was soaring gradually downwards and outwards. He was no longer afraid. He just felt a bit dizzy. Then he flapped his wings once and he soared upwards. He uttered a joyous scream and flapped them again. He soared higher. He raised his breast and banked against the wind. 'Ga, ga, ga. Ga, ga, ga. Gaw-ool-ah.' His mother swooped past him, her wings making a loud noise. He answered her with another scream. Then his father flew over him screaming. Then he saw his two brothers and his sister flying around him curveting and banking and soaring and diving.

Then he completely forgot that he had not always been able to fly, and commenced himself to dive and soar and curvet, shrieking shrilly.

He was near the sea now, flying straight over it, facing straight out over the ocean. He saw a vast green sea beneath him, with little ridges moving over it, and he turned his beak sideways and crowed amusedly. His parents and his brothers and sister had landed on this green floor in front of him. They were beckoning to him, calling shrilly. He dropped his legs to stand on the green sea. His legs sank into it. He screamed with fright and attempted to rise again, flapping his wings. But he was tired and weak with hunger and he could not rise, exhausted by the strange exercise. His feet sank into the green sea, and then his belly touched it and he sank no farther. He was floating on it. And around him his family was screaming, praising him, and their beaks were offering him scraps of dog-fish.

He had made his first flight.

A SHILLING

Three old men were sitting on the splash wall of Kilmillick Pier with their backs to the sea and their faces to the village and the sun. A light breeze came from the sea behind them, bringing a sweet salt smell of seaweed being kissed by the sun. The village in front was very quiet. Not a movement but the lazy blue smoke curling slantwise from the cabin chimneys. It was early afternoon, Sunday and all the young men and women were in Kilmurrage at a football match. The three old men were telling stories of big fish they had caught in their youth. Suddenly there was a swish of canvas and a little white yacht swung around the corner of the pier and came alongside. The three old men immediately got to their feet and advanced through the turf dust to the brink of the pier looking down at the yacht. Patsy Conroy the most active of the old men seized the mooring rope and made the yacht fast. Then he came back and joined the other two watching the yachtsmen getting ready to go ashore. 'She's lovely a boat', said old Brian Manion, the old fellow with the bandy right leg and the bunion behind his right ear. 'Heh', he said scratching the small of his back, 'it must cost a lot of money to keep that boat. Look at those shiny brasses and ye can see a carpet laid on the cabin floor through that hatchway. Oh boys!'

'I'd like to have her for a week's fishing', said Mick Feeney, breathing loudly through his long red nose. His big red-rimmed blue eyes seemed to jump in and out. He gripped the top of his stick with his two hands and looked down at the yacht with his short legs wide apart.

Patsy Conroy said nothing. He stood a little apart with his hands stuck in his waist-belt. Although he was seventy-two, he was straight, lithe and active, but his face was yellow and wrinkled like old parchment and his toothless red gums were bared in an old man's grin. His little eyes beneath his bushy white eyebrows roamed around the yacht cunningly as if they were trying to steal something. He wore a yellow muffler wound round and round his neck up to his chin, in spite of the heat of the day.

'Where is the nearest public-house?' drawled a red-faced man in a white linen shirt and trousers from the yacht deck.

44

The old men told him, all together.

'Let's go and have a drink, Totty', said the red-faced man.

'Right-o', said the other man.

When the red-faced man was climbing the iron ladder on to the pier a shilling fell out of his hip pocket. It fell noiselessly on a little coil of rope that lay on the deck at the foot of the ladder. The red-faced man did not notice it and he walked up the pier with his friend. The three old men noticed it, but they did not tell the red-faced man. Neither did they tell one another. As soon as the shilling landed on the little coil of rope and lay there glistening, the three of them became so painfully conscious of it that they were bereft of the power of speech or of coherent thought. Each cast a glance at the shilling, a hurried furtive glance, and then each looked elsewhere, just after the manner of a dog that sees a rabbit in a bush and stops dead with one paw raised, seeing the rabbit although his eyes are fixed elsewhere.

Each old man knew that the other two had seen the shilling, yet each was silent about it in the hope of keeping the discovery his own secret. Each knew that it was impossible for him to go down the iron ladder to the deck, pick up the shilling and ascend with it to the pier without being detected. For there was a man who wore a round white cap doing something in the cabin. Every third moment or so his cap appeared through the hatchway and there was a noise of crockery being washed or something. And the shilling was within two feet of the hatchway. And the old men, except perhaps Patsy Conroy, were too old to descend the ladder and ascend again. And anyway each knew that even if there were nobody in the cabin, and even if they could descend the ladder, that the others would prevent either one from getting the shilling, since each preferred that no one should have the shilling if he couldn't have it himself. And yet such was the lure of that glistening shilling that the three of them stared with palpitating hearts and feverishly working brains at objects within two feet of the shilling. They stared in a painful silence that was loud with sound as of a violent and quarrelsome conversation. The noise Mick Feeney made breathing through his nose exposed his whole scheme of thought to the other two men just as plainly as if he explained it slowly and in detail. Brian Manion kept fidgeting with his hands, rubbing the palms together, and the other two heard him and cursed his avarice. Patsy Conroy alone made no sound, but his very silence was loud and stinking to the other two men, for it left them in ignorance of what plans were passing through his crafty head.

45

And the sun shone warmly. And the salt, healthy smell of the sea inspired thirst. And there was excellent cool frothy porter in Kelly's. So much so that no one of the three old men ever thought of the fact that the shilling belonged to somebody else. So much so indeed that each of them felt indignant with the shameless avarice of the other two. There was almost a homicidal tendency in the mind of each against the others. Thus three minutes passed. The two owners of the yacht had passed out of sight. Brian Manion and Mick Feeney were trembling and drivelling slightly at the mouth.

Then Patsy Conroy stooped and picked up a pebble from the pier. He dropped it on to the deck of the yacht. The other two men made a slight movement to intercept the pebble with their sticks, a foolish unconscious movement. Then they started and let their jaws drop. Patsy Conroy was speaking. 'Hey there', he shouted between his cupped hands.

A pale-faced gloomy man with a napkin on his hip stepped up to the second step of the hatchway. 'What d'ye want?' he said.

'Beg yer pardon, sir', said Patsy Conroy, 'but would ye hand me up that shilling that just dropped out a' me hand?'

The man nodded, picked up the shilling, muttered 'catch' and threw the shilling on to the pier. Patsy touched his cap and dived for it. The other two old men were so dumbfounded that they didn't even scramble for it. They watched Patsy spit on it and put it in his pocket. They watched him walk up the pier, sniffing out loud, his long, lean, grey-backed figure with the yellow muffler around his neck, moving as straight and solemn as a policeman.

Then they looked at each other, their faces contorted with anger. And each, with upraised stick, snarled at the other:

'Why didn't ye stop him, you fool?'

THREE LAMBS

Little Michael rose before dawn. He tried to make as little noise as possible. He ate two slices of bread and butter and drank a cup of milk, although he hated cold milk with bread and butter in the morning. But on an occasion like this, what did it matter what a boy ate? He was going out to watch the black sheep having a lamb. His father had mentioned the night before that the black sheep was sure to lamb that morning, and of course there was a prize, three pancakes, for the first one who saw the lamb.

He lifted the latch gently and stole out. It was best not to let his brother John know he was going. He would be sure to want to come too. As he ran down the lane, his sleeves, brushing against the evergreen bushes, were wetted by the dew, and the tip of his cap was just visible above the hedge, bobbing up and down as he ran. He was in too great a hurry to open the gate and tore a little hole in the breast of his blue jersey climbing over it. But he didn't mind that. He would get another one on his thirteenth birthday.

He turned to the left from the main road, up a lane that led to the field where his father, the magistrate, kept his prize sheep. It was only a quarter of a mile, that lane, but he thought that it would never end and he kept tripping among the stones that strewed the road. It was so awkward to run on the stones wearing shoes, and it was too early in the year yet to be allowed to go barefooted. He envied Little Jimmy, the son of the farm labourer, who was allowed to go barefooted all the year round, even in the depths of winter, and who always had such wonderful cuts on his big toes, the envy of all the little boys in the village school.

He climbed over the fence, leading into the fields and, clapping his hands together, said, 'Oh, you devil', a swear word he had learned from Little Jimmy and of which he was very proud. He took off his shoes and stockings and hid them in a hole in the fence. Then he ran jumping, his bare heels looking like round brown spots as he tossed them up behind him. The grass was wet and the ground was hard, but he persuaded himself that it was great fun.

Going through a gap into the next field, he saw a rabbit

nibbling grass. He halted suddenly, his heart beating loudly. Pity he hadn't a dog. The rabbit stopped eating. He cocked up his ears. He stood on his tail, with his neck craned up and his fore feet hanging limp. Then he came down again. He thrust his ears forward. Then he lay flat with his ears buried in his back and lay still. With a great yell Little Michael darted forward imitating a dog barking and the rabbit scurried away in short sharp leaps. Only his white tail was visible in the grey light.

Little Michael went into the next field, but the sheep were nowhere to be seen. He stood on a hillock and called out 'Chowin, chowin', three times. Then he heard 'Mah-m-m-m' in the next field and ran on. The sheep were in the last two fields, two oblong little fields, running in a hollow between two crags, surrounded by high thick fences, the walls of an old fort. In the nearest of the two fields he found ten of the sheep, standing side by side, looking at him, with their fifteen lambs in front of them also looking at him curiously. He counted them out loud and then he saw that the black sheep was not there. He panted with excitement. Perhaps she already had a lamb in the next field. He hurried to the gap leading into the next field, walking stealthily, avoiding the spots where the grass was high, so as to make less noise. It was bad to disturb a sheep that was lambing. He peered through a hole in the fence and could see nothing. Then he crawled to the gap and peered around the corner. The black sheep was just inside standing with her fore feet on a little mound.

Her belly was swollen out until it ended on each side in a sharp point and her legs appeared to be incapable of supporting her body. She turned her head sharply and listened. Little Michael held his breath, afraid to make a noise. It was of vital importance not to disturb the sheep. Straining back to lie down he burst a button on his trousers and he knew his braces were undone. He said, 'Oh, you devil', again and decided to ask his mother to let him wear a belt instead of braces, same as Little Jimmy wore. Then he crawled farther back from the gap and taking off his braces altogether made it into a belt. It hurt his hips, but he felt far better and manly.

Then he came back again to the gap and looked. The black sheep was still in the same place. She was scratching the earth with her fore feet and going around in a circle, as if she wanted to lie down but was afraid to lie down. Sometimes she ground her teeth and made an awful noise, baring her jaws and turning her head around sideways. Little Michael felt a pain in his heart in pity for her, and he wondered why the other sheep didn't come to keep her company. Then he wondered whether his mother had felt the same pain when she had Ethna the autumn before. She must have, because the doctor was there.

Suddenly the black sheep went on her knees. She stayed a few seconds on her knees and then she moaned and sank to the ground and stretched herself out with her neck on the little hillock and her hind quarters falling down the little slope. Little Michael forgot about the pain now. His heart thumped with excitement. He forgot to breathe, looking intently. 'Ah', he said. The sheep stretched again and struggled to her feet and circled around once stamping and grinding her teeth. Little Michael moved up to her slowly. She looked at him anxiously, but she was too sick to move away. He broke the bladder and he saw two little feet sticking out. He seized them carefully and pulled. The sheep moaned again and pressed with all her might. The lamb dropped on the grass.

Little Michael sighed with delight and began to rub its body with his finger nails furiously. The sheep turned around and smelt it, making a funny happy noise in its throat. The lamb, its white body covered with yellow slime, began to move, and presently it tried to stand up, but it fell again and Little Michael kept rubbing it, sticking his fingers into its ears and nostrils to clear them. He was so intent on this work that he did not notice the sheep had moved away again, and it was only when the lamb was able to stand up and he wanted to give it suck, that he noticed the sheep was lying again giving birth to another lamb. 'Oh, you devil', gasped Little Michael, 'six pancakes.'

The second lamb was white like the first but with a black spot on its right ear. Little Michael rubbed it vigorously, pausing now and again to help the first lamb to its feet as it tried to stagger about. The sheep circled around making low noises in her throat, putting her nostrils to each lamb in turn, stopping nowhere, as giddy as a young schoolgirl, while the hard pellets of earth that stuck to her belly jingled like beads when she moved. Little Michael then took the first lamb and tried to put it to suck, but it refused to take the teat, stupidly sticking its mouth into the wool. Then he put his finger in its mouth and gradually got the teat in with his other hand. Then he pressed the teat and the hot milk squirted into the lamb's mouth. The lamb shook its tail, shrugged its body, made a little drive with its head and began to suck.

Little Michael was just going to give the second lamb suck, when the sheep moaned and moved away again. He said 'chowin, chowin, poor chowin', and put the lamb to her head, but she turned away moaning and grinding her teeth and stamping. 'Oh, you devil', said Little Michael, 'she is going to have another lamb.'

The sheep lay down again, with her fore leg stretched out in front of her and, straining her neck backwards, gave birth to a third lamb, a black lamb.

Then she rose smartly to her feet, her two sides hollow now. She shrugged herself violently and, without noticing the lambs, started to eat grass fiercely, just pausing now and again to say 'mah-m-m-m'.

Little Michael, in an ecstasy of delight, rubbed the black lamb until it was able to stand. Then he put all the lambs to suck, the sheep eating around her in a circle, without changing her feet, smelling a lamb now and again. 'Oh, you devil', Little Michael kept saying, thinking he would be quite famous now, and talked about for a whole week. It was not every day that a sheep had three lambs.

He brought them to a sheltered spot under the fence. He wiped the birth slime from his hands with some grass. He opened his penknife and cut the dirty wool from the sheep's udder, lest the lambs might swallow some and die. Then he gave a final look at them, said, 'Chowin, Chowin', tenderly and turned to go.

He was already at the gap when he stopped with a start. He raced back to the lambs and examined each of them. 'Three she lambs', he gasped. 'Oh, you devil, that never happened before. Maybe father will give me half-a-crown.'

And as he raced homeward, he barked like a dog in his delight.

THE WREN'S NEST

It was a summer's evening just before sunset. Little Michael and Little Jimmy, both twelve-year-old boys, set out to look for birds' nests. They were both dressed alike, except that Little Michael's blue sweater and grey flannel trousers were of better quality than Little Jimmy's, since the latter was the son of a farm labourer and Little Michael's father was the magistrate and a retired army officer. They were both barefooted, with cuts on their toes, and each had a bandage on the big toe of the right foot. They skirmished along south of the village, crossing the crags, picking berries and talking about the nests they had. No use looking for a nest until one came to the hollow there beyond Red Dick's potato garden. There was a cliff there over-looking a grassy glen. The cliff was awfully hard to climb and so was unexplored, and there was where they were going to search. It would be a great feat to climb the cliff anyway, since the only person who had climbed it was Black Peter, the bird catcher, and of course he was sold to the devil and could do anything. No boy had ever been able to climb it beyond the little ledge about a quarter of the way up, a ledge that was always covered with bird dirt and discoloured with cliff water that dripped on to it from a spring in the cliff face.

The two boys came to the cliff face and looked up. Then they looked at one another, their mouths open. 'You go first', said Little Michael. 'No, you go', said little Jimmy. 'No, you go.' They argued a long time about it, but neither moved. "Aw', said Little Michael, 'I think it's too late to climb it anyway to-day. Let us wait until to-morrow, and put on stockings. Black Peter always wears stockings. Stockings stick to the cliff face.' 'You're afraid', said Little Jimmy, wiping his nose with the sleeve of his coat. 'Who is afraid? My father fought in ten battles.' 'Climb it, then.' 'All right, let's climb it together.' 'Then who'll watch. We might be caught. Your father would summon me. That's certain.' They kept silent for a minute and then lay on their stomachs on the grass looking up at the cliff. Sparrows were chirping hidden in the ivy. Right at the top, about sixty feet above the level of the glen, there was a deep slit in the cliff and several broods of starling were croaking there.

'There must be twenty nests there', said Little Michael.

'There are forty. I counted them the other day', said Little Jimmy. 'Let's throw stones at them.' They threw a few stones up into the ivy and a number of birds flew out screaming. Then they lay down again on the grass and watched. Suddenly Little Jimmy said 'Hist!' His dirty face was lit up with sudden excitement. 'What's that?' whispered Little Michael. 'Hist!' said Little Jimmy, 'I see a wren. Look.' He pointed to a point far down in the cliff about five feet from the ground, where just a shred of ivy was growing, an offshoot from the main growth farther up. Little Michael nearly shut his eyes looking closely and saw a little brown ball moving slightly. The two boys held their breaths for a long time, lying quite still. Presently a tiny head peered out of the ivy. Then it disappeared again. Then it appeared again, looked around, and presently a wren flew out, circled around a little and landed on the fence to the left. Then it chirped lowly and sped away. Another little wren came out of the cliff in answer to the chirp and followed it.

'It's a nest', gasped both the boys together. They jumped to their feet and raced to the cliff, each trying to get there first.

They arrived at the cliff together and each thrust a hand into the little clump of ivy to get at the nest. There was a rustle of green leaves, a panting of breaths, and then their hands met in the ivy and they paused. They looked at one another and there was poisoned hatred in their eyes. 'I got it first', said Little Michael. 'I touched it first.' 'Ye're a liar', said Little Jimmy, 'I saw the wren first.' 'You call me a liar and your father was in jail twice.' 'I can beat you. I beat Johnny Derrane, and he beat you.'

'Oh, you just try.' They stood back from the cliff and looked one another up and down, each afraid of the other. The situation was intensely embarrassing, but just then one of the wrens flew back over the fence carrying a little wisp of moss in its mouth and saved the situation. They both looked at the wren, and said 'Hist!' glad of some excuse to prevent them from fighting. The wren alighted on a fence to the left and became very busy pretending to have a nest in the fence. 'Come away', said Little Michael, 'if he sees us looking at the nest he will forsake it, and a forsaken nest doesn't count. That's well known.'

'Oh, let's see how many eggs in it', said Little Jimmy. 'Nobody will believe us if we can't say how many eggs in it.' 'You leave it alone', said Little Michael; 'that's my nest. If you look at it, I'll tell my father.' 'Ha, spy', said Little Jimmy. Little Michael became very conscious of having made a fool of himself and didn't know what to say or do. He had an impulse to hit Little Jimmy, but he was afraid to hit him. No use fighting anyway when nobody was looking. Nobody ever heard of anybody fighting when there was nobody looking, unless two brothers maybe, or a boy and his sister. 'Maybe you think I'm afraid', he said at last. 'Take care now, Little Jimmy, that you'd think I'm afraid.'

'Aw, I don't care', said Little Jimmy, dabbing his toe into the grass with a swagger. 'I'm going to look at this nest anyway.' He moved forward and Little Michael caught him by the two hands and they struggled. 'Let me go', cried Little Michael. 'You let me go', cried Little Jimmy. The two wrens were now hovering about screaming in an agonized state, but the boys took no heed of them. Each was trying to grab at the nest and the other trying to prevent him. The ivy was soon torn from the cliff and a little round hole became visible, a beautiful little round hole, suggestive of beauty within, and around the little round hole was a house built of moss. Then Little Jimmy grabbed at the nest caught it in the tips of his fingers, and as Little Michael pulled him suddenly, the nest came out of the niche and tumbled to the ground. It fell on the ground on its side and a little egg, a tiny egg, tumbled out. It was so light that it landed between two blades of grass and stayed there poised. The wrens on the fence set up a terrible chatter and then flew away high above the ground. They would never come back.

The two boys looked at the nest in silence. 'Now see what you've done', said Little Michael; 'the nest is no use to us.' 'It's all your fault', said Little Jimmy; 'you were afraid to look at it.' 'Who was afraid?' said Little Michael heatedly; 'what do I care about a wren's nest', and he kicked the nest with his foot. The structure of dried moss burst in two pieces and several eggs scattered around. Both boys laughed, and began to kick the pieces of the nest and then tore them to shreds. The inside was coated wonderfully with feathers and down, interlaced with an art that could not be rivalled by human beings. The boys tore it into shreds and scattered the shreds. Then they pelted one another with the eggs, laughing excitedly. Then they paused, uncertain what to do, and they both sighed, from satisfaction. They were friendly again, the cause of their quarrel had vanished, destroyed by their hands.

'I got a rabbit's nest with three young ones in it', said Little Jimmy.

'Show it to me', said Little Michael, 'and I'll show you a blackbird's nest with three eggs in it,' 'All right', said Little Jimmy, and they scampered off, over the fence where the wrens flew away. Two fields farther on they passed the wrens, already looking for another niche, but they did not recognize them. If they had they would probably have thrown a few stones at them.

THE BLACK MARE

I bought the mare at G—, from a red-whiskered tinker and, if
the truth were only known, I believe he stole her somewhere in
the south, for he parted with her for thirty shillings. Or else it
was because she was so wild that there was not another man at
the whole fair had the courage to cross her back with his legs
and trot her down the fair green but myself, for it was not for
nothing that they called me Dan of the Fury in those days.
However, when I landed from the hooker at the pier at Kilmurrage and, mounting her, trotted up to the village, they all
laughed at me. For she was a poor-looking animal that day,
with long shaggy hair under her belly, and the flesh on her ribs
was as scarce as hospitality in a priest's house. She didn't stand
an inch over fourteen hands, and my legs almost touched the
ground astride of her. So they laughed at me, but I paid no heed
to them. I saw the fire in her eyes, and that was all I needed.
You see this drop of whiskey in this glass, stranger? It is a pale,
weak colour, and it would not cover an inch with wetness, but it
has more fire in it than a whole teeming lake of soft water. So
the mare.

I set her to pasture in a little field I had between two hills in
the valley below the fort. I cared for her as a mother might care
for an only child, and all that winter I never put a halter in her
mouth or threw my legs across her back, but I used to watch
her for hours galloping around the fields snorting, with her
great black eyes spitting fire and her nostrils opened so wide
that you could hide an egg in each of them. And, Virgin of the
Valiant Deeds, when she shed her winter coat in spring and I
combed her glossy sides, what a horse she was! As black as the
sloes they pick on the slope of Coillnamhan Fort, with never a
hair of red or white or yellow. Her tail swept to the ground, and
when the sun shone on her sides you could see them shimmering like the jewels on a priest's vestments; may the good God
forgive me, a sinner, for the comparison. But what is nearer to
God than a beautiful horse? Tell me that, stranger, who have
been in many lands across the sea.

And then the day came when all the unbroken mares of
Inverara were to be shod. For it was the custom then, stranger,

to shoe all the young mares on the same day, and to break them before they were shod on the wide sandy beach beneath the village of Coillnamhan.

There were seven mares that day gathered together from the four villages of Inverara, and there were good horses among them, but none as good as mine. She was now a little over fifteen hands high, and you could bury a child's hand between her haunches. She was perfect in every limb, like a horse from the stable of the God Crom. I can see her yet, stranger, standing on the strand stamping with her hind leg and cocking her ears at every sound. But it's an old saying, talk of beauty to-day, talk of death to-morrow.

I kept her to the last, and gave her to a lad to hold while I mounted a bay mare that my cousin had brought from Kilmillick, and I broke her in three rounds of the strand, although she had thrown three strong and hardy men before I seized her halter. And then my mare was brought down, and then and there I offered three quarts of the best whiskey that could be bought for money to the man that could stay on her back for one length of the strand. One after the other they mounted her, but no sooner did they touch her back than she sent them headlong to the ground. She would gather her four legs together and jump her own height from the ground, and with each jump they flew from her back, and she would run shivering around again until they caught her. I smiled, sitting there on a rock.

Then Shemus, the son of Crooked Michael, spat on his hands, tightened his crios around his waist, and said that if the devil were hiding in her bowels and Lucifer's own step-brother riding on her mane, he would break her. He was a man I never liked, the same son of Crooked Michael, a braggart without any good in him, a man who must have come crooked from his mother's womb, and his father before him was the same dishonest son of a horse-stealing tinker. 'Be careful', I said to him; 'that mare is used to have men about her that didn't drink their mother's milk from a teapot.' And when I saw the ugly look he gave me I knew that there was trouble coming, and so there was.

He got up on her all right, for, to give the devil his due, he was agile on his limbs and, although no horseman, there were few men in the island of Inverara that he couldn't throw with a twist of the wrist he had. But as soon as his legs rubbed her flanks she neighed and gathered herself together to spring, and just as she was that way doubled up he kicked her in the mouth with his foot. She rose to her hind legs and before she could

56

plant her fore feet on the ground again to jump, I had rushed from the rock and with one swing of my right arm I had pulled him to the ground. I was so mad that before he could rush at me I seized him by the thigh and the back of the neck, and I would have broken every limb in his putrid body if they didn't rush in and separate us. Then the craven son of a reptile that he was, as soon as he saw himself held, he began to bellow like a young bull wanting to get at me. But I took no heed of him. My father's son was never a man to crow over a fallen enemy.

They brought the mare over to me and I looked at her. She looked at me, and a shiver passed down her flank and she whinnied, pawing the sand with her hind hoof.

'Take off that halter', said I to the men.

They did. I still kept looking at the mare and she at me. She never moved. Then coming over to her as she stood there without saddle or bridle, stepping lightly on my toes, I laid my right hand on her shoulder. 'Pruach, pruach, my beautiful girl', I called to her, rubbing her shoulders with my left hand. Then I rose from the strand, leaning on the strength of my right hand and landed on her back as lightly as a bird landing on a rose bush. She darted forward like a flash of lightning from a darkened sky. You see that strand, stretching east from the rock to where it ends in a line of boulders at the eastern end. It is four hundred paces and it rises to the south of the boulders into a high sand bank underneath the road. Well, I turned her at the sand bank with a sudden flash of my hand across her eyes, leaning out over her mane. And then back again we came, with a column of sand rising after us and the ground rising up in front of us with the speed of our progress. 'Now', said I to myself, 'I will show this son of Crooked Michael what Dan of the Fury can do on horseback.'

Raising myself gently with my hands on her shoulders, I put my two feet square on her haunches and stood straight, leaning against the wind, balancing myself with every motion of her body, and as she ran, stretched flat with her belly to earth, I took my blue woollen shirt off my back and was down again on her shoulders as light as a feather before we reached the western end, where the men stood gaping as if they had seen a priest performing a miracle. 'God be with a man', they cried. And the women sitting on the hillock that overlooks the beach screamed with fear and enjoyment, and of all the beautiful women that were gathered there that day there was not one that would not have been glad to mate with me with or without marriage.

Back over the strand again we went, the black mare and I,

like lightning flying from the thunder, and the wave that rose when we passed the rock in the west had not broken on the strand when we turned again at the sand bank. Then coming back again like the driven wind in winter I rose once more, standing on her haunches, and may the devil swallow me alive if I hadn't put my shirt on my back again and landed back on her shoulders before we reached the rock. There I turned her head to the sea and drove her out into it until the waves lapped her heaving belly. I brought her back to the rock as gentle as a lamb and dismounted.

Ha! My soul from the devil, but that was a day that will never be forgotten as long as there is a man left to breathe the name of Dan of the Fury. But all things have their end, and sure it's a queer day that doesn't bring the night, and the laugh is the herald of the sigh. It was two years after that I got this fractured thigh. Well I remember that four days before the races where I got this broken limb, I met red-haired Mary of Kilmillick. As I was looking after her, for she had shapely hips and an enticing swing in them, my horse stumbled, and although I crossed myself three times and promised to make a journey to the Holy Well at Kilmillick, I'll swear by Crom that the spell of the Evil One was put on the mare. But that is old woman's talk. Mary promised me the morning of the races that if the black mare won, I could put a ring on her finger, and as I cantered up to the starting point I swore I would win both the race and the girl if the devil himself were holding on to the black mare's tail.

Seventeen horses lined up at the starting point. I took up my position beside a bay stallion that the parish priest Fr. John Costigan, had entered. He was a blood stallion and had won many races on the mainland, but the parish priest was allowed to enter him, for who could go against a priest. Then, as now, there was nobody in Inverara who was willing to risk being turned into a goat by making a priest obey the rules of a race. Six times they started us and six times we were forced to come back to the starting point, for that same braggart, the son of Crooked Michael, persisted in trying to get away before the appointed time. At last the parish priest knocked him off his horse with a welt of his blackthorn stick and the race started.

We were off like sixteen claps of thunder. We had to circle the field three times, that big field above the beach at Coill-namhan, and before we had circled it the second time, the bay stallion and the mare were in front with the rest nowhere. Neck to neck we ran, and no matter how I urged the mare she would not leave the stallion. Then in the third round of the field I caught a sight of Mary looking at me with a sneer on her face, as if she thought I was afraid to beat the priest's horse. That look drove me mad. I forgot myself. We were stretching towards the winning post. The stallion was reaching in front of me. Mad with rage I struck the mare a heavy blow between the ears. I had never struck her in my life and as soon as I had done it I started with fright and shame. I had struck my horse. I spoke to her gently but she just shivered from the tip of her ears to her tail and darted forward with one mighty rush that left the stallion behind.

I heard a shout from the people. I forgot the blow. I forgot the mare. I leaned forward on her mane and yelled myself. We passed the winning post, with the stallion one hundred yards or more behind us. I tried to draw rein. Her head was like a firm rock. I cursed her and drew rein again. I might have been a flea biting her back. At one bound she leapt the fence and swept down the beach. She was headed straight for the boulders. I saw them in front of me and grew terrified. Between us and the boulders was the sand bank, fifteen feet high. She snorted, raised her head and tried to stop when she saw the fall. I heard a shout from the people. Then I became limp. We rose in the air. We fell. The mare struck the rocks and I remembered no more.

They told me afterward that she was shattered to a pulp when they found us, and sure it's the good God that only gave me a broken leg.

SPORT: THE KILL

With a wild rush of scraping feet, the rabbit darted in under the flat rock. His right hind leg spat up a sliver of stone from the crag and disappeared, just as the dog's snout landed with a thud at the hole. The dog yelped as he tumbled head over heels with the force of his mad rush. The rabbit crawled along the straight groove in the crag under the rock. His claws made a rasping sound as, one after the other, his legs thrust his body forward. He left a trail of brown fur behind him. Midway he halted, panting. He saw the dog's black nose twitching and snorting at the far end of the groove in front. He painfully drew up his legs under his belly, twisted around his head so that he could see both entrances to the groove and waited. His sides pressed against the rock as they heaved.

A boy came bounding along from the left, skipping over the boulders that lined the cliff top. In his right hand he carried a dried long willow rod. He halted on a boulder and looked about him. The dog raised his head, looked at the boy, wagged his tail and barked. The boy whooped and rushed along the crag to the rock. The dog growled joyously and, throwing back his head, he scraped madly at the hole, clawing the limestone crag impotently. The boy threw himself flat at the other end where the rabbit had entered, shut one eye and looked in. When his eye pierced the gloom and he saw the rabbit, he too growled.

The rabbit, seeing enemies on both sides, tried to stick his head through a tiny crevice to his left, where the rock rested on two cone shaped spurs of the crag. His head entered as far as the ears and could go no farther. He lay still, one ear bent double, the other ear flat on his back, the tip quivering, fanned by the dog's breath, that came through the damp groove in a pale blue column. Then a scratching sound reached him, coming towards his hind-quarters. The boy lying on his side was pushing the dried willow rod along the groove.

The end of the rod touched the rabbit's left haunch gently. It slipped up over the haunch and tipped the rock. Then it twisted with a grating sound and got stuck in the soft fur to the left of the tail. It twisted again. The skin on the rabbit's haunches went taut as it gathered around the tip of the rod. The rabbit started, held his breath and pulled his head suddenly from the

60

crevice. He was stretching back his right leg to crawl away from the rod when he saw the dog's red tongue lolling between white fangs at the far end in front of him. With his right hind leg crooked at the thigh, he paused, his eyes blinking, his whiskers twitching, his ears pressed down into his contracted neck. Again the rod grated and twisted. The skin of his stomach was drawn up to the ball of skin and fur that was gathering around the tip of the rod. Again the rod twisted. The skin around his crutch went taut.

The boy cursed. A spur of the crag had bruised his hip. He grunted and said 'Hs-s-s-s' fiercely. The dog thrust his muzzle abruptly at the hole and barked. The bark re-echoed through the groove and the fur on the rabbit's neck quivered. The rabbit closed his eyes and bent down his head. The strong smell of the dog's breath was stifling him. Then the boy drew in a deep breath and tried to twist the rod again. His sweating hands slipped on the dried willow. The rod was too taut to turn. All the skin on the rabbit's body was as taut as the skin of a drum. The claws of his right hind leg gripped the crag with such force that their points were blunted. The dog raised his head and walked back a few paces to smell a snail that was crawling along the crag. Then he came back to the hole again, raised his left fore paw and cocked his head sideways.

Slowly, carefully, the boy began to pull the rod. For a few moments the pressure was so gradual that the rabbit did not feel himself being pulled. Then suddenly his right hind leg that was bearing the weight of his body slipped backwards with a scraping sound that ended in a thud. His whole body began to slip, bumping against the crag, the fore feet pawing the ground. He allowed himself to slip back gradually, too dazed to resist. The dog sniffed cautiously at his hole. Then fiercely. He thought the rabbit was escaping. Darting across the rock to the boy, he yelped and thrust his snout down between the boy's face and the hole. Then he whined and darted back again to his own hole.

The rabbit was within a foot of the boy's hand at the mouth of the hole when the rod caught in a cleft, where the rock rested on a spur of the crag just within the mouth of the groove. The boy cursed and gave the rod a jerk. It failed to move. Then he pushed it back. The rabbit drew up his hind legs under him feeling the tension relaxed. Then the boy tried to give the rod another twist to free it. He had twisted it around slightly when the skin on the rabbit's haunch burst with a snap. The rabbit jerked his head up and down suddenly and, striking the crag with his four feet, thrust himself forward with a wild squeal.

61

The dog thrust his body at his hole furiously, cutting his muzzle against the crag. Then he lay on his belly, his eyes watery, his jaws slightly open. The boy jumped to his knees and, seizing the rod with both hands, he wrenched it clean out of the groove with a large patch of the rabbit's skin at its tip. The rabbit blinded by the pain crawled straight ahead heedless of the dog. The dog drew back his snout. His tail stretched out. His eyes half closed. His chest shivered. The rabbit's head appeared. There was a smothered squeal and then a low crack as the dog's fangs met through the rabbit's neck.

The dog tossed the rabbit in triumph over his head as the boy leaped across the rock. The boy grabbed the rabbit's hind legs and kicked the dog fiercely on the ribs. The dog dropped the rabbit and ran back whining. The boy held up the body heaving as if it were leaping fences in its death agony. 'High' he hissed through his teeth.

Then he bashed the rabbit's head on the rock.

THE SNIPER

mood setting

The long June twilight faded into night. Dublin lay enveloped
in darkness, but for the dim light of the moon, that shone
through fleecy clouds, casting a pale light as of approaching
dawn over the streets and the dark waters of the Liffey. Around
the beleaguered Four Courts the heavy guns roared. Here and
there through the city machine guns and rifles broke the silence
of the night, spasmodically, like dogs barking on lone farms.
Republicans and Free Staters were waging civil war.

On a roof-top near O'Connel Bridge, a Republican sniper lay
watching. Beside him lay his rifle and over his shoulders were
slung a pair of field-glasses. His face was the face of a student –
thin and ascetic, but his eyes had the cold gleam of a fanatic.
They were deep and thoughtful, the eyes of a man who is used to
looking at death.

He was eating a sandwich hungrily. He had eaten nothing
since morning. He had been too excited to eat. He finished the
sandwich, and taking a flask of whiskey from his pocket, he
took a short draught. Then he returned the the flask to his
pocket. He paused for a moment, considering whether he
should risk a smoke. It was dangerous. The flash might be seen
in the darkness and there were enemies watching. He decided to
take the risk. Placing a cigarette between his lips, he struck a
match, inhaled the smoke hurriedly and put out the light.
Almost immediately a bullet flattened itself against the parapet
of the roof. The sniper took another whiff and put out the
cigarette. Then he swore softly and crawled away to the left.

Cautiously he raised himself and peered over the parapet.
There was a flash and a bullet whizzed over his head. He
dropped immediately. He had seen the flash. It came from the
opposite side of the street.

He rolled over the roof to a chimney stack in the rear, and
slowly drew himself up behind it, until his eyes were level with
the top of the parapet. There was nothing to be seen – just the
dim outline of the opposite housetop against the blue sky. His
enemy was under cover.

Just then an armoured car came across the bridge and
advanced slowly up the street. It stopped on the opposite side of
the street fifty yards ahead. The sniper could hear the dull

panting of the motor. His heart beat faster. It was an enemy car. He wanted to fire, but he knew it was useless. His bullets would never pierce the steel that covered the grey monster.

Then round the corner of a side street came an old woman, her head covered by a tattered shawl. She began to talk to the man in the turret of the car. She was pointing to the roof where the sniper lay. An informer.

The turret opened. A man's head and shoulders appeared, looking towards the sniper. The sniper raised his rifle and fired. The head fell heavily on the turret wall. The woman darted toward the side street. The sniper fired again. The woman whirled round and fell with a shriek into the gutter.

Suddenly from the opposite roof a shot rang out and the sniper dropped his rifle with a curse. The rifle clattered to the roof. The sniper thought the noise would wake the dead. He stopped to pick the rifle up. He couldn't lift it. His forearm was dead. 'Christ', he muttered, 'I'm hit.'

Dropping flat on to the roof, he crawled back to the parapet. With his left hand he felt the injured right forearm. The blood was oozing through the sleeve of his coat. There was no pain – just a deadened sensation, as if the arm had been cut off.

Quickly he drew his knife from his pocket, opened it on the breastwork of the parapet and ripped open the sleeve. There was a small hole where the bullet had entered. On the other side there was no hole. The bullet had lodged in the bone. It must have fractured it. He bent the arm below the wound. The arm bent back easily. He ground his teeth to overcome the pain.

Then, taking out his field dressing, he ripped open the packet with his knife. He broke the neck of the iodine bottle and let the bitter fluid drip into the wound. A paroxysm of pain swept through him. He placed the cotton wadding over the wound and wrapped the dressing over it. He tied the end with his teeth.

Then he lay still against the parapet, and closing his eyes, he made an effort of will to overcome the pain.

In the street beneath all was still. The armoured car had retired speedily over the bridge, with the machine gunner's head hanging lifeless over the turret. The woman's corpse lay still in the gutter.

The sniper lay for a long time nursing his wounded arm and planning escape. Morning must not find him wounded on the roof. The enemy on the opposite roof covered his escape. He must kill that enemy and he could not use his rifle. He had only a revolver to do it. Then he thought of a plan.

64

not a person, just the "enemy."

Taking off his cap, he placed it over the muzzle of his rifle. Then he pushed the rifle slowly upwards over the parapet, until the cap was visible from the opposite side of the street. Almost immediately there was a report, and a bullet pierced the centre of the cap. The sniper slanted the rifle forward. The cap slipped down into the street. Then, catching the rifle in the middle, the sniper dropped his left hand over the roof and let it hang, lifelessly. Afer a few moments he let the rifle drop to the street. Then he sank to the roof, dragging his hand with him.

Crawling quickly to the left, he peered up at the corner of the roof. His ruse had succeeded. The other sniper seeing the cap and rifle fall, thought that he had killed his man. He was now standing before a row of chimney pots, looking across, with his head clearly silhouetted against the western sky.

The Republican sniper smiled and lifted his revolver above the edge of the parapet. The distance was about fifty yards – a hard shot in the dim light, and his right arm was paining him like a thousand devils. He took a steady aim. His hand trembled with eagerness. Pressing his lips together, he took a deep breath through his nostrils and fired. He was almost deafened with the report and his arm shook with the recoil.

Then, when the smoke cleared, he peered across and uttered a cry of joy. His enemy had been hit. He was reeling over the parapet in his death agony. He struggled to keep his feet, but he was slowly falling forward, as if in a dream. The rifle fell from his grasp, hit the parapet, fell over, bounded off the pole of a barber's shop beneath and then cluttered on to the pavement.

Then the dying man on the roof crumpled up and fell forward. The body turned over and over in space and hit the ground with a dull thud. Then it lay still.

The sniper looked at his enemy falling and he shuddered. The lust of battle died in him. He became bitten by remorse. The sweat stood out in beads on his forehead. Weakened by his wound and the long summer day of fasting and watching on the roof, he revolted from the sight of the shattered mass of his dead enemy. His teeth chattered. He began to gibber to himself, cursing the war, cursing himself, cursing everybody.

He looked at the smoking revolver in his hand and with an oath he hurled it to the roof at his feet. The revolver went off with the concussion, and the bullet whizzed past the sniper's head. He was frightened back to his senses by the shock. His nerves steadied. The cloud of fear scattered from his mind and he laughed.

Taking the whiskey flask from his pocket, he emptied it at a draught. He felt reckless under the influence of the spirits. He decided to leave the roof and look for his company commander to report. Everywhere around was quiet. There was not much danger in going through the streets. He picked up his revolver and put it in his pocket. Then he crawled down through the sky-light to the house underneath.

When the sniper reached the laneway on the street level, he felt a sudden curiosity as to the identity of the enemy sniper whom he had killed. He decided that he was a good shot whoever he was. He wondered if he knew him. Perhaps he had been in his own company before the split in the army. He decided to risk going over to have a look at him. He peered around the corner into O'Connell Street. In the upper part of the street there was heavy firing, but around here all was quiet.

The sniper darted across the street. A machine gun tore up the ground around him with a hail of bullets, but he escaped. He threw himself downwards beside the corpse. The machine gun stopped.

Then the sniper turned over the dead body and looked into his brother's face.

TWO DOGS

Feeney, the fisherman, had two dogs. One was a mongrel, a black dog, deep-chested and ferocious. The other was a yellow greyhound, thin and beautiful. The two dogs were deadly enemies. The mongrel was five years old when Feeney bought the greyhound as a pup. Before the greyhound's arrival the mongrel shared his little cottage with Feeney, followed him each day to the cliffs to fish and hunted rabbits. Whenever he killed one, which was not very often, because he was not fast, he brought it in his mouth to Feeney and wagged his tail proudly. He was very fond of Feeney, and he was quite happy. Everybody feared his ferocity, and all the dogs in his own village and along the countryside fled when they saw him coming.

Then the pup came to the cabin, and the mongrel was no longer happy. He hated to see Feeney fondle it and feed it with milk, while he himself had to be content with potatoes and rockfish heads. He would sit on his haunches watching the long-legged pup sniff around the floor or tear at Feeney's trouser leg, and whenever he got a chance he bit at him. But Feeney beat him whenever he bit the pup and he often had to lie on his back and allow the young greyhound to tear at his throat fur and gambol over him. He would yawn savagely and loll his tongue, unable to satiate his rage.

Then the pup grew up and began to accompany Feeney to the cliffs to fish. He was still growing and ugly, and whenever a strange dog came near him he threw himself on his back and whined. So the mongrel despised him and felt sure Feeney would not prefer such an ugly cowardly creature to himself. One day Feeney beat the young greyhound for running away from a mangy terrier that was blind in one eye, and the mongrel was quite happy. He began to snap at the greyhound in the presence of his master without being interfered with. The young greyhound began to hate the mongrel and grew madly jealous of his deep chest, his strength, and his courage.

Then the greyhound grew to his full size, and he was beautiful to look at. He was almost twice the mongrel's height, and his snout was so long and pointed that he could lick milk from the bottom of a tumbler without touching the sides. His yellow

67

coat was as glossy as silk, and he could outdistance anything. Almost without moving a muscle, he could jump from a standing position and go clean over Feeney's head without touching it. Feeney was delighted with him, and all the neighbours stopped to praise him, so that the mongrel grew vicious with jealousy and took to howling at nights, until Feeney had to get up one night and give him a stiff thrashing with a broom handle.

But when the rabbit season came in again the mongrel turned the scales against the greyhound. The greyhound was slow to pick up a scent and could not follow one when he did get one. So while the mongrel methodically nosed along the rabbit's trail, the greyhound rushed about furiously, mad with excitement, jumping stone walls with his head in the air and absolutely useless. Then when the mongrel started the rabbit, the greyhound outdistanced him in a few strides, but was unable to catch the rabbit because of his own terrific speed and the rocky ground, which cut his delicate paws and made him stumble. And it always happened that the hound turned the rabbit into the mongrel's mouth, for the mongrel was old and cunning and knew his ground perfectly and the habits of rabbits. He knew when to follow over a fence and when to wait behind. He knew which side a rabbit would turn and when he was going to turn. So that he caught all the rabbits and the hound caught none. Nearly every day he came to the cliff-top with a rabbit in his mouth and dropped it beside Feeney. Then he would gambol about, make a savage rush at the greyhound, and come back again barking joyously as much as to say, 'There's that useless greyhound'. Feeney began to think the greyhound was worthless and took a dislike to him. When the greyhound crawled up to him and put his head under his armpit after a kill by the mongrel, Feeney gave him a sharp blow on the side with his bait hammer and sent him away.

Then one summer morning, just after dawn, when the rocks were still shimmering with evaporating dew and there was such a freshness in the silent air that it made each living thing throb with joy at the very fact of living, Feeney was going along up the slope of Coillnamhan Fort towards his usual fishing perch on the cliff-top. The two dogs were rushing about over the crags mad with the joy of early morning, sniffing at every hole and making desperate rushes at hummocks of grass, pretending that they concealed a rabbit. And at last the mongrel started one two fields below the cliffs, at the base of a steep slope that ended in the brink of a precipice that dropped two hundred and fifty feet to the sea. The greyhound was some distance behind, but the rabbit went through a hole in a high fence, and while the mongrel was running to a low part to jump, the greyhound cleared the high fence without touching it and got in the lead. The next field was very craggy, and the greyhound fell twice and cut himself in several places, so that the rabbit reached the next fence before the greyhound could get up to him. That fence was a low one, and the greyhound took it at a flying leap and landed in front of the rabbit. The rabbit turned back into the field he had just left and was going through the hole just as the mongrel was jumping the fence. The greyhound doubled back over the fence and turned the rabbit once more, and the mongrel, who had cunningly waited the cliff side of the fence, tried to grab at the rabbit when he came through the hole the second time. But his foot caught in a crevice and he missed him. The rabbit raced up the grassy slope to his burrow on the cliff-top. The mongrel ran after him. The greyhound doubled back again over the fence with his head in the air and his tongue hanging. He whined and raced up the slope with his nose to the ground. Feeney threw down his basket and began to yell.

The mongrel suddenly saw the cliff-top and slowed down and began to bark. But the greyhound flew past him like a thunderbolt, and nosed the rabbit just as he was going to dip around the little rock at the cliff-top into his burrow. There was a muffled yelp from the hound and a scream from the rabbit, as they both went whirling over the cliff to the sea two hundred and fifty feet below. The mongrel ran up to the brink of the cliff and looked down. He sniffed and let his ears droop. Then he began to bark joyfully and run around trying to catch his tail.

THE HOOK

The seagull was very hungry. He was soaring above the fishing village with his legs hanging down, his wings perfectly still, his head turned to one side and his sharp little eyes blinking. Above him and a little to the right, a large white flock of seagulls was cackling and diving about furiously. He alone was sailing on his own, very near the ground and perfectly silent. He saw something that he didn't want the other seagulls to see until he should get an opportunity of securing it for himself.

There it was, perched enticingly on a low stone fence, the fat red liver of a fish, about three inches long and as thick as it was long. The seagull ravened for it. He would swoop down immediately and bite at it, but he wanted to bring a share to his mate that was sitting on the eggs, on the ledge in the cliff. So he was waiting for an opportunity to rest for a moment on the fence, eat his own share and take the rest between his beak northwards to the cliff.

But he could not get an opportunity. The fence on which the liver rested bordered the lane that led from the well to the wide flat crag where the village women were washing and cleaning and salting the fish that had been caught the previous night. Young girls continually passed along the lane carrying buckets of water to their mothers. And the seagull was slightly bewildered by all the noise and bustle on the crag, with the women in their red petticoats and little black shawls around their heads squatted on their heels, and their sharp knives making the white scales fly in little flaky showers from the fishes' backs. Their harsh cries, the flashing of the knives in the bright morning sun, the glittering piles of fish slipping about, all made the seagull's head swim with excitement and hunger and desire and fear.

At last he heard a hoarse 'ga-ga-ga' close by him and another seagull swooped past the fence where the liver rested and then, banking a little farther on, doubled back, cackling aggressively as he came. The first seagull knew that the liver was discovered. He must wait no longer. He swooped upwards slightly, flapped his wings twice and then came straight down with a tearing sound. He landed lightly on the fence, took fright suddenly and looked about him, uttered a queer faint shriek and was going to spread his wings to fly again when he heard a swish and the other seagull landed beside him. The first seagull lost all fear, grabbed at the liver and tried to swallow the whole piece. He got it into his mouth in two gobbles, while the other seagull picked at its end and screamed. Then with a wild yell a number of small boys who had been hiding under the fence a few yards to the right, jumped up and began to wave their arms. The second seagull screamed and darted away. The first seagull made a last violent gobble at the liver and got it completely in his mouth and then with a fierce swing of his wings he rose sideways.

But he did not rise far. With a smothered scream he came tumbling backwards. A hook had been hidden in the liver. Its barb was sticking through the seagull's mouth, in the soft part behind the lower bill, and a piece of string protruded from his mouth and was tied to a stone in the fence. The seagull was trapped.

He fell with wings outstretched inside the fence. He lay dumbfounded for two seconds, lying on his side, his little eyes motionless with fear and pain. Then a boy leaned over the fence and tried to grab at him. He fluttered away a yard or so to the full reach of the string and then when the hook jerked him back again, he uttered a fierce cry as if spurred to madness by the renewal of pain. Bending his head he rose with the graceful and powerful movement of an advancing wave. He rose in a twirling curve. There was a slight snap, a downward jerking of his beak, then he uttered a joyful scream like a loud sigh and he flew upwards with a curling piece of string hanging from his beak. He had burst the string and left the small boys staring after him and cursing the weak string that had robbed them of their prey.

Higher and higher he whirled, upwards from the village and northward towards his ledge on the cliff and his mate. As he whirled and banked and plunged forward the string kept dangling and going through funny little convolutions, as if it were a long worm being carried off and trying to wriggle its way out of the seagull's mouth. And the whole flock of seagulls followed the hooked one, making a tremendous noise, screaming at one another and blinking their little eyes in amazement at the hook sticking from the trapped one's bill and the string dangling.

At last the seagull reached his ledge midway down a precipitous cliff. The sea grumbled far away beneath, and as his mate sat on her eggs her bill protruded over the sea, the ledge was so narrow. The trapped seagull landed beside his mate. She wearily stretched out her beak for food and then uttered a wild

71

scream as she saw the hook. And breasting the ledge the whole flock soared about cackling. The trapped one, stupefied by all the cackling, hid one leg under his wing and let his head fall until the tip of his bill touched the ground. A little drop of blood trickled along the bill and fell on the rock.

Then the female bird seized the string in her beak and, without rising from her eggs, she began to tear at it furiously, cackling shrilly the while, like a virago of a woman reviling a neighbour. The wounded bird sank down on his breast and let his head go limp, while the whole flock of birds hovered nearer and became more subdued with their cries. Some landed on neighbouring ledges and craned their necks to watch the female bird's furious pecking.

Soon the string was cut. Then she seized the hook by the barb that protruded from beneath the bill. She pulled. The male bird spluttered a cry and flapped his wings, but the female bird arched her neck and wrenched again. The hook came with her almost. But its circular end with the string tied to it remained in the male's beak. A little stream of blood ran out. Then the male bird, unable to endure the pain any longer, tried to wrench himself clear. He pulled backwards fiercely and left the hook in his mate's bill. There was wild and victorious cackling as the freed bird staggered to his feet, shook his beak, and uttering a weak, plaintive, surprised scream, dipped it into a little pool of water on the ledge.

His mate lay back on her eggs, smoothed her feathers with a shrug and closed her eyes in a bored fashion.

THE WILD SOW

Old Neddy the fisherman, of Kilmillick, bought a sow pig one day in Kilmurrage. He put the pig in a bag, dropped in into one of his donkey's creels and brought it home to his cabin. It was just six weeks old, a little black pig, with a long back, and big ears that dropped over its eyes and a little tail curled up in a knot.

The neighbours were surprised when they heard that Neddy had bought the pig, for he was an old man and lived alone in his two-roomed cabin and he had no land except a little patch in front of his door that grew enough potatoes to last him the year round. He was, too, very fond of drink, and whenever he had any money he stayed in Kilmurrage until he had spent it. So that the neighbours wondered what possessed him to buy the pig. In fact Martin Conroy came into Neddy's cabin and said, 'Brother, it's plain that they fooled you into buying that young pig, so if ye'll throw ten rockfish into the bargain with it, I'll give you a pound for it.'

Neddy hitched up his belt, glanced at Conroy with his little grey eyes and told him to get out of his cabin. Then he shook his fist after Conroy and said, 'I'll have money while I have that pig and that's why I bought it. So may the devil choke the lot of you.'

He made a straw bed for the little pig in the corner of his kitchen and sawed off the lower part of a barrel in which he salted his fish to make a trough for it. For a while he looked after it carefully and gave it plenty of potatoes, dry fish and whatever sour milk he could get from the neighbours. So that the sow got big and fat until it was six months old and fit for sale. But when a jobber came to look at it and asked Neddy what price did he want, Neddy told him to get out of his cabin. 'I have money', he said, 'while I have that pig, so I'll keep it.'

That was in the month of April and Neddy's stock of potatoes had been all eaten by the sow and most of his dried fish along with the potatoes, so he turned the sow loose on the roadside to eat grass, saying, 'Now feed yerself and may the devil choke you.' And he took his basket and his fishing lines and went away to fish.

The sow wandered about on the road all the forenoon,

smelling at everything, snorting furiously and making little short runs that made her foot joints snap under her fat body like hard biscuits being cracked, when a horse or a peasant driving a cow went past. She rooted among the grass until her head was caked with earth up to her eyes. Then towards her feeding time at midday she trotted back to the cabin, but the door was locked. For a time she waited at the door grunting and with her ears cocked listening to every sound, sniffing the air with her twitching hairy snout and tossing her head now and again in vexation. Then, when nobody opened the door, she began to whine with the hunger. She stood there motionless and whining until Neddy came back at dusk and let her into the cabin. He only gave her fish guts and potato peelings for her supper 'From now on', he said, 'you'll have to fend for yourself, and may the devil choke you.'

That went on for a fortnight with Neddy away fishing every day, and then the sow got thinner and wild with hunger. She began to eat grass by the roadside and roamed over the crags picking nettles and everything she could get hold of. She no longer snorted when horses or cows passed her. Her bristles grew rough and strong and her ears lost their tender transparency. Her eyes were hardly visible through the caked dirt that gathered around them. She used to run out of the cabin in the morning and never come near it again until dusk.

At first she roamed about the village of Kilmillick, eating grass and nettles, tearing up the ground for roots, chewing everything she found in rubbish heaps, old fish bones, rags, boots and potato skins. Then, as the summer grew, the heat and the long days tempted her farther, down to the beach and along the lanes and the road leading to Kilmurrage. Often she never came back to the cabin for two or three days at a stretch, but would spend the night among the sandhills about the beach where the wild grass was very sweet and there was always a dog-fish or a piece of mackerel cast up by the sea among the weeds. Her bristles were now as stiff and thick as needles, and her black skin beneath them was cracked by the sun and scarred in places where dogs bit her or boys struck her with stones and dried sea rods when they cornered her in narrow lanes. All her flesh had hardened into muscle. She was lean like a hound and nearly as tall as a year-old donkey.

Towards the end of summer a jobber came again to Neddy and asked him would he sell the sow. 'She's not much good now', said the jobber, 'so I'll give ye a pound for her. I might be able to soften her a bit and get a litter from her.' 'Get out of my cabin', said Neddy, 'and may the devil choke you. I have money while I have that pig, so I'll keep the pig.' But the fishing was bad that year and he had to sell his donkey in order to buy flour for the winter. Still he wouldn't sell the pig. 'It's like having money in a bank', he would say, 'a pig is always money. I often heard my father say so.'

But when winter came on and the ocean winds swept the crags viciously and sea foam was falling like snow over the cabins, the sow could go out no more, but sat on her haunches on her straw litter in Neddy's kitchen grunting and whining with the hunger.

Then one stormy day Neddy went into Kilmurrage to sell his dried pollock. He turned the pig out of the cabin and locked the door. Then he went away. The sow roamed about for a while shivering with the cold and weak with hunger. Her stomach was drawn up into her back so that she looked like a cat that is stretching itself. She could discover nothing to eat around the village so she came back to the cabin.

She got on her knees at the door and began to gnaw at the bottom until she made a hole for her snout; then she seemed to go mad and tore at the door with her teeth and battered it with her head until she burst it off its hinges and she pushed right under it into the cabin. The door hung on one hinge and the sow's right ear was gashed down the middle by a nail in the jamb.

She stood in the middle of the kitchen grunting, with her snout to the ground and with blood dripping from her ear in a steady stream. Then she tossed her head and rushed at Neddy's bedroom door. Sticking her snout at the bottom near the jamb, she pushed and burst the string with which the door was fastened and got into the bedroom. Neddy's potatoes were lying in the far corner with a little wall of stones around them. His sack of flour stood against the wall near the potatoes. His dried rockfish were stacked on pieces of paper under the wooden bedstead. The sow began to eat. Snorting and tossing her head she ran from the flour to the potatoes and then to the rockfish, swallowing huge mouthfuls without chewing, and making a noise like a horse pulling her hoof out of a bog, until her stomach swelled out to a point at each side.

Then a big potato stuck in her throat.

When Neddy came in that evening he found her lying on her side, stone dead.

A POT OF GOLD

It was a moonlight night in July. The sky was very big, blue and silent. The valley of Rossmore, lying between towering rocky mountains that rose on either side of it, was peaceful. It was covered with a light grey mist, calm, as if it slept. A very long way off frogs croaked in a marsh.

Just before midnight four men came up the lane from the hamlet of Rossmore, going towards Mount Simon. As they crossed the flat stretch of hunchbacked moor, through which the lane ran before it reached the foot of the mountain road, they halted. They had been walking, owing to the narrowness of the lane, in single file. John Gillan, who was in front, pulled up suddenly and then the other three, one by one, had to halt suddenly, thrown one on top of the other, with their hands thrust out in front of them to protect themselves from falling, panting with terror of the weird, silent night and of the sombre, empty mountainside.

John Gillan was a thickset man, wearing a raincoat that had been washed to a whitish colour and reached from his throat to the insteps of his black heavy boots. A black slouch hat fell about his face. The moonlight shone on his fat red face and on his long grey beard as he turned sideways to talk to Barney Rogers who came behind him. Leaning on a light crowbar he held in his two hands with its end resting on the grass, he bent his head and whispered. 'Have ye got the black-handled knife?' he said.

Barney Rogers was a slight, tall, young man, dressed in an old blue suit, with the coat reaching down to the middle of his thighs in Irish fashion and a grey tweed cap perched at the back of his curly black head. He was so thin that the cartilages in his neck were visible as he strained forward his head towards Gillan. His little grey eyes opened wide and his little snub nose quivered. He clapped his hand on his left trousers pocket, felt the pocket and then he whispered: 'Sure I have. Here it is under my hand.'

'Make sure', whispered Gillan. 'It's very important, the black-handled knife. We're not safe without it.'

'Here she is', whispered Rogers pulling out a little black-handled pocket-knife. 'Ye can see for yerself.'

Gillan crouched down and peered at the handle. The other two men crowded around, with a swishing noise of heavy boots coming through grass. The three men, breathing loudly and murmuring, bent down, feeling the knife handle and peering at it. Rogers, with his head and shoulders outlined in the moonlight above the stooping forms of the other three men, winked both eyes and wrinkled up his face at the sky, as if he were bursting with suppressed laughter.

'She is black, sure enough', said Gillan at length.

'She is', whispered the other two men. They were two brothers called Higgins and they worked on Gillan's farm. They were big men dressed in grey frieze trousers and blue jerseys. They stood with their mouths open and a wild look in their black eyes. The two of them carried hammers in their hands.

Rogers carried nothing in his hands. He was a stone-cutter. He lived alone in a little cabin and he was rather a notorious character.

The four of them moved off again in single file, Gillan leading. They turned to the left, along the road that went up the side of Mount Simon until it reached the Reservoir. About half-way up Rogers said 'Hist' and tapped Gillan on the right shoulder. Gillan stopped with a start and looked behind him sideways.

'We leave the road here and turn on to the crags to the left', whispered Rogers. 'The rock is within two hundred yards of here.'

Gillan took off his hat and blessed himself. The Higgins brothers did likewise, murmuring the prayer aloud as they crossed themselves. After a little pause Rogers also took off his cap and blessed himself.

'Let's sit down for a minute', said Gillan.

'We had better open the bottle', said Rogers.

'Very well', said Gillan, 'but mind, it's to be only a short swig.'

He fumbled within his raincoat and took out a quart bottle of whiskey. The four of them crouched under the little low stone fence as if they were hiding from something. The moon shone brightly on the white narrow road, the grey fence and the mountain side getting blacker and blacker as it faded away in the distance. Gillan had drawn the cork in the house but he was fooling with it a long time before he could draw it again. At last it came out with a soft sound. The sweet fragrance of the whiskey rushed out into the still night air.

They all drank, Gillan first. Then Gillan put the bottle back. The Higgins brothers kept peering over the top of the fence to the left with their mouths open. Gillan buttoned up his raincoat and then gripped Rogers by the left knee. Rogers was kneeling on his right knee with his left knee doubled up and his elbow resting on it.

'Now are ye sure ye dreamt of it three nights running?' said Gillan.

'As sure as I have an immortal soul', whispered Rogers fiercely, taking off his cap and holding it with both hands to his breast. 'Three nights running I've seen that flat rock with red moss growing on a corner of it. Then the rock is raised up in the dream and there is a dead black cat lying under it and then down below that again, down far into the ground, through the rocks, there is a black iron pot on three legs and that pot is full of gold sovereigns. Full to the brim and the top ones are rusty.'

Gillan and the two Higgins brothers listened with awe.

'Can ye say how far down the pot is?' said one Higgins, the one called Pat, a man with large red ears, and warts on his hands.

'Shut yer mouth, Pat Higgins', hissed Gillan, angry that his farm labourer should ask questions on the matter in his presence. 'Can't ye see that I'm talkin'?' he added arrogantly after a pause. Then he turned to Rogers and said in a stern tone: 'Now look here, Barney Rogers. Ye've made me buy a quart bottle of the best whiskey and ye've brought me out here at dead of night, to the danger of my immortal soul with believing in yer dreams, so, be the Cross of Macroom, if yer fooling me about the rock and the cat and the pot of gold ... well, ye may look out for yerself. That's all. Come on, men. You go ahead, Rogers. Lead the way to yer rock.'

To the left of the road the side of the mountain was bare and broken. Limestone rocks, deeply creviced, protruded everywhere unevenly, with here and there a little clump of withered heather or grass. The ground was jagged in places. They walked slowly. Several times Rogers halted, holding up his hand behind him to the others. Then he would bend down on his hands and knees examining the ground about him. At last he said, 'Ha!' excitedly and darted forward to a little eminence. The eminence was crowned by an oblong flat rock.

'Exactly as in my dream', cried Rogers, getting down on his two knees on a little bunch of withered heather beside the rock. He took off his cap with one hand and pointed to the rock with the other. 'Look at the red moss', he whispered to Gillan.

Gillan's voice died in his throat as he tried to say something. Then he nodded his head and got on one knee beside Rogers, holding the crowbar upright in his right hand. The Higgins brothers sat on their heels with their hammers in their hands and their mouths open. They kept darting their eyes around in terror. All kept silent for several seconds. Their breathing was loud in the silence. The sound of each man's breath was distinct from the others, with the four sounds mingling irregularly. Gillan's shadow fell across the rock, his long beard sticking across the short shadow of the crowbar.

'Let's have another drink before we begin', whispered Rogers at last.

In silence Gillan took out the bottle and uncorked it. When the cork came out with a flop the Higgins brothers started violently. All drank. Gillan took off his raincoat and rolled the bottle in it.

'In the Name of God', he said, 'let's begin. Are we to break the rock or turn it?'

'Turn it, turn it', said Rogers. 'You three turn it. I'll stand here with the black-handled knife in my hand.'

Rogers stood up, opened his knife and, holding it out in front of his body in his right hand, he said: 'Now turn it.' The three men, brushing against one another roughly, gripped the rock and heaved with all their might. The rock skidded and turned a complete somersault off its bed. All looked at the bed.

A dead black cat lay stretched there, with his yellow eyes open.

The Higgins brothers yelled and ran over the crags to the road, their heavy boots slipping among the stampeding cattle. Gillan had not screamed, but he jumped back and he put his hand to his throat and gripped his chest, just above the pit of his stomach, with the other hand. Just there his Scapular of the Sacred Heart was hanging on a cord. He murmured a prayer. Rogers stood behind and it was impossible to see the expression on his face in the darkness. He made no sound. At last Gillan spoke.

'It's the black cat', he whispered, 'he's there. D'ye see him?'

'I see him', whispered Rogers. 'It's him sure enough. There he lies, just as he lay in the dream guarding the treasure.'

'How are we going to get him out of it?' asked Gillan fearfully. 'Who is going to touch him and maybe be burned alive, Lord between us and all harm.'

'I'll do it', said Rogers, 'I'll do it. Give me the bottle. It'll be the devil to touch him.'

'There, take a good drink', said Gillan, handing him the bottle.

Rogers took a long swig. Then he rested, smacking his lips.

Then he took another swig. Gillan, excited and looking at the cat, took no notice of him. Rogers cast a glance at Gillan and then he hastily put the bottle to his head again, took a little hurried swig and rammed in the cork. The two Higgins brothers arrived back just then, walking on their toes, with their hands raised outwards like men walking a tight rope. Gillan shook his fist at them and scowled for some reason or other.

Rogers stood up, holding the black-handled knife open in his right hand. With a sudden movement he swept his cap from his head and threw it from him to the ground. Gillan and the two brothers watched every movement breathlessly. Then, holding the knife over the cat, Rogers stooped down and grasped it by the tail. He lifted the tail. The cat came up, stiff and flat like a pancake. There was a burnt spot, a spot as big as a shilling, on the cat's left side below the shoulder. Pat Higgins, staring wild-eyed at the cat, saw the yellow spot and started slightly. Then he shivered and looked at Gillan. Rogers walked away five paces on tiptoe and then placed the cat gently on the ground. Then he wiped his forehead with the back of his hand and came back to Gillan, looking exhausted.

'Yer a brave man, Barney', whispered Gillan in an awed tone.

'Give me . . . a drink', mumbled Rogers, dropping on one knee and wiping his forehead.

He took the bottle in his hand and pulled the cork. Then he turned to Gillan and said: 'Now it's safe for ye to go ahead and dig. But be careful. If ye see a bone or a feather don't touch it. Tell me and I'll take away the spell with my knife. I'll sit here and watch, for fear the cat 'd change into a devil and burn ye alive. As long as I keep looking at him with the whiskey in me hand, he is helpless. Now hurry up and begin to dig.'

'Right', cried Gillan excitedly, standing up.

'Come on, men', he hissed; 'get to work and bend yer backs to it. I'll loosen the stones with the crowbar.'

Under the flat rock the stones were small and loose for about six inches, and under that there were thin layers of stone with black earth in between. The three men, panting and perspiring, cleared away the loose stones and then Gillan began to dig the layers with his crowbar and the two Higgins brothers tore away the loosed stones with their hands, breaking one now and again with their hammers. Rogers, kneeling on one knee with the open bottle in his hand, asked now and again, 'D'ye see any sign of the pot?' and as each time Gillan replied that he didn't, Rogers said, 'Work harder', and he took another swig at the bottle.

Gillan dug like a madman, his eyes gleaming avariciously down into the hole. Already he pictured himself digging his hands into the golden sovereigns, clutching handfuls of them.

Then suddenly Rogers held up the bottle to the moonlight. It was half empty. He glanced around him hurriedly, and bared his teeth in a grin. He got to his feet. He moved away towards the road three paces backwards. Then he paused and called out: 'Dig, dig, something tells me ye are within a foot of the pot. Dig, dig like hell.' Then he turned and ran on his toes like a deer to the road without making a sound. If he made as much noise as a tramcar the three men digging would not have heard him at that moment. Then Rogers vaulted the low fence into the road and disappeared.

The three men worked away for a long time. At last Pat Higgins paused to take breath and looked behind him at the spot where Rogers was kneeling. He started and nudged Gillan. Gillan turned about and looked where Higgins was pointing. Rogers had disappeared. Soon the three of them had dropped their tools and were standing about, looking everywhere with wonder in their face, silently. Nobody spoke for at least a full minute. At last Pat Higgins swore out loud and clenched his fists.

'What is it, you fool?' cried Gillan angrily.

'It's my Aunt Mary's cat', yelled Higgins. 'Ye've been made a fool of, John Gillan. I know the yellow spot on his side now. Oh, by the . . .' and he began to swear a terrible string of oaths as he rushed over to the old dead black cat and lifted him up. There was the same yellow burnt spot. They all looked at it.

Gillan raised his clenched fists above his head and stuttered, unable to speak with rage.

'Three days ago the cat disappeared and nobody knew what happened to him. It's how Rogers killed him. He should be arrested for it.'

'Arrested', yelled Gillan, suddenly becoming articulate and turning on Higgins, 'd'ye want my name all over the county? Don't speak a word of this or I'll have yer lives. Don't give it to say to the dirty illegitimate son of a tramp that he made a fool of me. Oh, holy mother of God, how am I going to live the shame and disgrace of it?'

All the way home he kept wringing his hands and crying aloud.

THE FIGHT

Black Tom, a peasant, leaned against the counter of Mulligan's public-house. In spite of his large mouth being open, his breath going in and out through his nostrils sounded like steam hissing from a kettle. His upper teeth stuck out. A lock of hair hung down over his forehead beneath his tam-o'-shanter cap. All his bones and limbs were awkward and he was so tall that he looked slim. Nobody knew how tall he was. He must have been six feet and three inches.

As he leaned against the counter, his body seemed to be melting like snow, it looked so loosely knit together, and he changed his weight from leg to leg restlessly. His dim blue eyes strained wide open, stared stupidly at the counter. He was very drunk. It was the first time he had been drunk in six months. He had sold a pig at the fair in Kilmurrage for five pounds. He gave four pounds to his wife and told her to go home. She begged for the fifth, so he had to give her a few cuffs on the ear to get rid of her. Then he had drunk six pints of Guinness's porter in Mulligan's.

'Another pint', he said to the barmaid, and as he spoke he hiccupped. Then he heard somebody laugh behind him, and wheeling around cumbersomely, like a horse carrying a great weight, he saw his enemy Bartly Sweeney enter the bar with two friends. He tried to think why Bartly Sweeney was his enemy, and for the life of him he could not remember why he was, but he felt certain that he was. So he said 'Hello Bartly, hello there, boys, what are ye havin'?'

Each of the three men wiped his mouth and said, 'Mine is a pint!' Bartly Sweeney a square young man in a grey frieze trousers and blue sweater with a horsewhip stuck in his belt, spat on his hand and took Black Tom's in his.

'How are you, Tom?' he said.

'Fine, how's yerself?' said Tom, trying to smile and only succeeding in looking stupid, like a child looking at a stranger.

The barmaid brought Black Tom his fresh pint and he ordered three more for Sweeney and his friends. Sweeney began to talk to the barmaid, bantering her, and then Black Tom drew in a great breath that almost burst his nostrils, they swelled so much. He knew at that moment why Sweeney was his enemy. He was jealous of Sweeney, because Sweeney was a good-looking fellow and a great favourite among the women. It was common knowledge that Kitty Cooney, Black Tom's wife, was in love with Sweeney before she married Black Tom. Perhaps she is in love with him yet, thought Black Tom, staring at his pint. He despised his wife, but it was another matter having her in love with Sweeney, perhaps having children by him, same as he had heard it said women did in the United States. And Sweeney had been in the United States.

He felt a sudden desire to hit Sweeney on the top of the head, but just then Sweeney turned to him laughing over something he had just said, and Black Tom laughed too, shifting his weight to his other leg, and spitting out with a great noise in his throat. He knew now that Sweeney had followed him in to fight him.

'Here's luck.' 'Good luck.' 'Long life.'

They all drank. While he had his pint to his lips Black Tom was seized with a sudden fury and finished his pint at a draught. He would show this fellow Sweeney that even though he was ugly and had two teeth sticking out over his lips, that he was a strong man and able to drink his liquor. He dropped his empty pint on the counter with a bang, wiped his mouth with the back of his hand and tightened his belt, but nobody took any notice of him.

Sweehey was still talking to the barmaid and the other two men were listening to him. Black Tom felt irritated because nobody took any notice of him. He looked at the barmaid. She was leaning on the counter on her elbows, with her head cocked slantwise. Her breasts nearly showed above the neck of her blouse, as they pressed against the counter and her elbows. Her fuzzy hair was neatly piled on her head and her cheeks were flushed, listening to Sweeney's jokes. Black Tom suddenly felt a desire for her. Why the devil had he not married her instead of Kitty Cooney? Why, Sweeney had all the women in the island after him, and he was not married at all. The dog. He looked at Sweeney.

Sweeney's sleek face was clean shaven and ruddy. His jaws were fresh and pink after the lather. The lines of his lips under his well-trimmed moustache were clear cut and regular. There was a nonchalant deviltry in his blue eyes, half covered by his eyelids. The very pose of his well-made body leaning far to the left was insulting. Black Tom could stand it no longer. He struck the counter with his clenched fist and roared. The barmaid started, put her hands to her throat and said 'Jesus, Mary, and Joseph.' But strangely enough, neither Sweeney nor his two friends took any notice whatsoever. Black Tom roared again. Sweeney turned around, put his hands under his armpits and looked at him. There was silence for three seconds. Black Tom was debating furiously in his mind what he should say to Sweeney.

'What's that ye said to me last year?' he screamed at last. 'Are ye as good a man now as ye were last year?'

Sweeney put his back to the counter and leaned an elbow on either side of him. Then he cracked the third finger and thumb of both hands.

'I don't care what I said last year or this year', said Sweeney.

There was silence for several seconds, while the two men stared furiously at one another. Then Black Tom stamped on the floor with his right foot and yelled again.

'There isn't a man in Inverara as good as me', he cried. 'I could beat all the measly, rat-whiskered, pock-marked sons of drunken priests in Kilmurrage with my little finger.'

Then he roared again and began slowly to unbutton his waistcoat, finding great difficulty in keeping himself steady on his feet.

'I'll tell you what's the matter with you', sneered Sweeney, his face set in a contemptuous grin. 'You need somebody to wipe your nose.'

Black Tom growled, stamped with both his feet, ground his teeth and moved back a pace to spring or something, and fell on his buttocks on an empty barrel. Then he commenced to howl as if he were weeping.

'I'm alone', he wailed, 'I'm alone among three of them, and there is nobody to hold my coat while I knock both the eyes out of his head. For God's sake, why don't somebody hold me back before I kill him.'

Then Sweeney seeing that his enemy was getting panic-stricken, tightened his belt around his waist, threw away his horsewhip, a penknife, three fishing hooks and an Agnus Dei. He stood in the middle of the floor and stamped with his right foot in a bellicose manner.

'I'm standing as God made me', he cried, addressing the barmaid with a conceited look in his eyes, 'and I haven't a weapon on me and no man is going to raise a hand to help me. And what's more I can knock the life out of any man that was ever conceived by a drunken father, and there's one present.'

The other two men sniggered and Black Tom, having by now exhausted all his rage against Sweeney, for by nature he was a good-tempered man, roared again to show everybody that he was not afraid. He jumped to his feet and with a final effort threw off his waistcoat. It fell on the counter and knocked down a pint. Everybody rushed to pick up the pint and everybody shouted 'Don't break the house.'

'I'll break everything', cried Black Tom, and, avoiding Sweeney, he rushed around the room hitting the walls with his head, biting the chairs with his teeth, kicking wildly. Sweeney moved over to the counter, eager to avoid coming into contact with him. The barmaid began to scream. The other two men, brave because they were not expected to fight, caught hold of Black Tom and tried to expostulate with him. But as soon as they seized him, Black Tom became really angry. He became savage. He became conscious of his great strength. He seized one of them in each hand and with one swing sent them crashing against the wall, where they fell in a heap. Then he rushed at Sweeney, but Sweeney stepped aside skilfully. Black Tom crashed against the counter, where he lay in a heap while Sweeney stood warily waiting with his fists doubled by his side. Black Tom lay on the counter for a long time. His brain began to work again. He became afraid. He felt that he was making a fool of himself. He might get arrested. What was Sweeney doing over there behind him?

Why were they all silent? He pretended to be very drunk, although he was now almost sober. He spluttered and hiccupped and threw his hands about him on the counter aimlessly. Then he struggled to an erect position, and pretending not to see Sweeney, tore at his shirt and blubbered, 'There isn't a man—'

Then Sweeney, nervous with fear that Black Tom was going to seize him and crush him to death in his mighty arms, hit him suddenly in the jaw and he fell in a heap to the floor.

After a while he came to his senses and heard them talking.

'Poor man', said the barmaid, 'there's no harm in him, only he loses his reason when he has a little drop taken.'

'Nobody was sayin' a word to him', said Sweeney.

'If it was anybody else threw me like that—' said one of the men.

Black Tom felt ashamed of himself, but he was too weak to assert his dignity by fighting. Instead he drank two glasses of whiskey hurriedly and left the public-house. On his way home he wept loudly. He would stand in the middle of the road and grind his teeth and swear that he would kill Sweeney some day.

When he got home he broke all the delph in the house. He whittled out a stick to thrash Sweeney and finally fell asleep on the hearth. Next morning he had a sick head when he went to work.

He did that twice every year.

WOLF LANIGAN'S DEATH

It was a frosty January night about ten o'clock. A large barge drawn by two horses was coming slowly down the Canal nearing its destination at Portobello Bridge, Dublin. There was no moon, but now and again glaring lights from the tramcars that rattled over the Bridge lit up the dark waters of the Canal, the grey bulk of the barge, the taut rope, the narrow gravel path and the two lean horses walking slowly in single file with their heads drooping.

Then as the barge drew closer to the bank, Wolf Lanigan raised his head and shoulders behind the windlass in the bows and looked about him cautiously. 'Jump, towny', cried the helmsman in a whisper. Wolf stood up suddenly, jumped on to the tarpaulin that covered the cargo, stooped and took a flying leap to the bank. He landed on his hands and knees, jumped to his feet, waved his hand to the barge and vaulted over the low concrete wall into the street beyond. He landed ankle deep in the mud beside the wall with a loud thud. The noise made him stiffen with his hands and back gripping the concrete wall. He listened for several seconds without breathing. Not a sound in the dark street but the squelching of the displaced mud. He ran crouching across the street and into a dark alleyway between two houses. At the far end there was a heap of rubbish and an upturned cart in a little wooden shed. He went on his hands and knees in the shed behind the cart, took an electric torch from the pocket of his loose raincoat and flashed it about. There was nothing but a heap of straw, a torn black hat lying in a corner, and an empty sack.

He switched off the torch and placed it in the cart. Then he took off his raincoat, a blue serge coat and a leather jacket. Lying between his shoulder blades on his white shirt was a Colt automatic pistol, bound by leather thongs around his neck and waist.

He loosed the thongs, placed the pistol in the cart, and dressed hurriedly. Then he switched on the torch again and placed it in the cart with the light towards him. He took the pistol, released the cartridge case, emptied the cartridges, wiped each one with a handkerchief, notched their heads with a clasp knife, returned them to the case and returned the case to the pistol. Then he switched off the light, put it in his pocket and jumped to his feet. He put the pistol in his left breast pocket, and with right hand on the butt he walked back into the street with stooping shoulders.

He crossed Dublin without stopping, following dark side streets, going under arches and through by-lanes. He passed over the Liffey at Butt Bridge and then hurried through a maze of slum streets until he reached Dublin's brothel quarter, north of Amiens Street. There he slackened his pace and went cautiously, stopping at every corner and convulsively pressing the butt of his pistol when anybody passed. At last he crossed a waste patch of ground that was strewn with bricks, heaps of debris and old pots and he came to the corner of Divis Street.

Peering around the corner of a deserted house at the end of the street a blaze of light struck him, running low to the ground in parallel lines until it ended in a dark lane at the far end. The light streamed from the open doorways of the two-storied brothels, shebeens, and dens of criminals on either side, while the second stories were in darkness, or with only a dim light showing through heavy blinds. The street was crowded with men and women, walking up and down and standing at the doorways, some drunk, staggering and quarrelling, others singing with clasped hands, others walking silently in couples with the measured tread of policemen. Strains of music and the sound of wild singing and still wilder laughter rose from the street in a strange inhuman melancholy roar to the still sky overhead. And yet in spite of the noise there seemed to be a deadly silence. The music, the singing, the banging of doors, the obscene curses, the drunken lascivious laughter came like a casual murmur heard from the bottom of a dark abyss.

The Wolf waited over five minutes, motionless, with his body pressed against the brick wall, watching the street. He could not move while those silent couples were pacing up and down steadily, seemingly intent on nothing but their thoughts. He knew their eyes would catch him slinking past, that guns would flash out, and deep voices bellow out 'hands up! . . .'

Then from the far end a young woman came staggering down the street, hanging on the arm of a young man. Her long black hair flowed down about her shoulders. A loose dressing-gown was open to below her breasts. She laughed hysterically as she tried to brandish a bottle over her head. Then suddenly another woman rushed out at her from an open doorway. 'Let him go, you b – , he's mine.' A shriek, a sudden rush and the two women were at one another's throats. The whole street gathered around, shouting. 'Now's my chance', muttered the Wolf.

He darted along the side of the street, passed the crowd and dived into a dark doorway at the far end. On tiptoe he passed a door on the right of the hall. Sounds of drunken revelry came through the door, sounds packed close together as of a pot boiling furiously. In the hall there was the silence and darkness of death. The Wolf drew his pistol and groped for the wall with his left hand. He couldn't see his hand. At last he found the wall. He slid along it, holding the pistol behind him, facing the street. His foot came in contact with a stairway. Noiselessly he mounted step after step, sideways, with the pistol behind. He reached a landing. The roof was so low that he had to stoop. Opposite him there was a gleam of light coming through the keyhole of a door. Catlike, lifting each foot carefully and planting it flat, he reached the door. He put his ear to the keyhole and listened. Then he knocked quietly, two double knocks. There was a noise of a bed creaking and then of slippers shuffling along a boarded floor. The door opened slightly and a woman's head appeared. 'Rosie', hissed the Wolf.

'God!' ejaculated the woman, stepping back.

The Wolf darted in after her and closed the door gently and put his back to it. Turning the key with one hand, with his gun levelled, his eyes darted around the room. It was bare, low roofed, garret-like, with a table in the centre of the bare boarded floor. On the table was a white cloth with dirty crockery in a pile at one end. In the corner was a wide bed with the yellow quilt crushed, evidently where the woman had been lying on top of it. A coal fire burned brightly in the open grate. A lamp with a broken chimney hung on a nail on the wall. Not a sound was heard in the room but the lazy crackling of the fire and the distant heavy murmur from the street coming through the heavy blinds on the window. The air was heavy and thick.

The Wolf stood with his legs wide apart, crouching forward from the hips. His sallow face was contorted with excitement. A thick growth of black beard covered his square jaws and his lips. There was a patch of clotted blood over his right eye. His boots were caked with mud and there was a large rent in his right trouser leg below the raincoat that covered his body from there to the throat. A grey tweed cap was pulled far down over his head. A bony hand covered with dirt gripped the pistol close to his hip. He stood squat, broad-shouldered, leaning forward, as if he were ready to jump through the window at the slightest sound.

The woman stood by the table staring at him with an expression of horror on her pale beautiful face. It was deadly pale. Even the open lips were pale and her large eyes were glassy and lifeless. A long plait of black hair was hanging over her right shoulder, trailing down the breast of her loose grey dressing-gown. Her hands clutched at the end of the plait. Her bare feet were stuck into a pair of heelless slippers. She stood, tall and motionless, staring wildly and intently at the Wolf's face, with compressed lips, as if hypnotized.

For several seconds they stood that way, the two of them, in the silent room. Then suddenly the Wolf spoke.

'Anybody been here?' His voice came in a hoarse, cracked whisper, the voice of a man who has spent sleepless nights in the winter air.

The woman tried to speak, swallowed something and shook her head.

'What the hell is the matter with ye?' hissed the Wolf through his yellow teeth. 'Aren't ye glad to see me? Eh! Has anybody been here? Ye know who I mean?'

He advanced towards her noiselessly and stood with the muzzle of his pistol pointed within an inch of her breast. But the woman, without a movement of her body and without taking her eyes from his face, just shook her head once more. Then she gasped, shivered, put her right hand to her forehead, and sank to a chair by the table, still looking at the Wolf, as if drawn by a magnet.

'Afraid of me? Eh?' said the Wolf opening his mouth wide and bursting into a noiseless laugh. His head and shoulders shook, but he made no sound. 'Do I look funny? Eh? Come on, move an' get me somethin' t' eat. I'm starved. D'ye hear? Didn't eat this two days. Move, blast ye.'

He watched the woman get to her feet and walk to the cupboard near the fireplace. Then he moved on the flat of his feet to a chair by the table facing the door. He laid the pistol in front of him. The woman was putting a kettle on the fire.

'Don't mind that kettle, I tell ye', he said. 'Give me somethin' t' eat. I don't want any tea. Haven't ye got any grub?'

Without a word she dropped the kettle and went back again to the cupboard. The Wolf took off his cap. His forehead was bald and sloped straight back from his eyes. There was another large patch of congealed blood where the bald spot met the hair near the top of his skull. He put his fingers to it and ground his teeth with pain. The woman put a pork pie, bread, butter and milk on the table. She moved mechanically, using only one hand, as if driven by an alien will to do something hateful. And all the time her lifeless eyes strayed to the Wolf's face. Without looking at her the Wolf began to eat ravenously. Every time a shout came from the street, he started, looked around wildly and grabbed his pistol. The woman stood by the fireplace, with her hands folded on her breast, motionless, her eyes fixed on his face.

Then he finished eating, licked his fingers and looked at the woman. His small grey eyes roamed over her face and his under lip protruded.

'Why the hell don't ye say somethin'?' he snarled. 'Ye heard about the racket in Mullingar, didn't ye?'

The woman's lips quivered, but she didn't speak. He jumped up, and gripped her by the right shoulder and pointed the gun at her breast.

'Listen to what I'm goin' to tell ye. I'm goin' to tell ye somethin' that'll wake ye up, dosey. D'ye know where I went four days ago? Eh? Well, me an' Chris Moloney an' the Bull Kelly went to raid a bank in Mullingar. The cops followed us from here, see? Somebody gev the game away. Chris an' the Bull got pinched, an' I'd have got pinched too, only I plugged a cop. I plugged a man, Rosie, d'ye hear? Shot him dead. Been two days comin' down in a canal boat. I'm wanted for murder, d'ye hear?'

The woman nodded her head several times and pointed to a newspaper that lay in the coal-scuttle. The Wolf darted over and picked it up. On the front page in large headlines it ran:

MULLINGAR BANK HOLD UP
DETECTIVE SERGEANT CARNEY SHOT DEAD

And underneath was the Wolf's photograph.

The Wolf swore softly, crushed the paper into a ball and stamped on it. Then he turned once more to the woman. His nostrils were expanding and contracting.

'Listen. They aren't goin' to get me by – ' He pulled out the cartridge case from the pistol. 'They are all dum-dum. An' one is for mesel' and another for you. See? The rest is for the gang that comes to take me. Un'erstan'?'

There were beads of sweat on his swarthy forehead. The woman never moved or spoke. But her eyes became larger and the skin around her lips tightened. Swearing frightfully the Wolf took a bottle of whiskey from the cupboard and held it up to the light. It was nearly full. He wrenched out the cork with his teeth and drank deeply. Then he sat down again at the table facing the door, his left hand clutching the bottle, his right on

91

his pistol butt. The woman drew a chair to the fire and sat down, still watching him. The Wolf began to drink, starting at every noise; and between drinks he stared at the table, his eyes narrowed, his forehead wrinkled into deep furrows, as if his brain were struggling with some intricate problem. The silence in the room was intense. Then gradually the Wolf's face relaxed. He began to move his limbs and nod his head. Then he struck the table with his fist, put the bottle to his head and emptied it and got to his feet. His body swayed slightly and there was a slight mist before his eyes. With his foot he drew his chair beside the woman's. He was careless now about making a noise. He sat down with a flop. He still had the gun in his hand. He put his arm around her waist. She looked into the fire and shivered.

'Say, Rosie.' His voice was loud and hoarse and there was an attempt at merriment in it. 'Be nice to me. Won't ye? Ain't I been a good pal to ye? Eh? Be the lumpin' Moses didn't I pick ye up in O'Connell Street half starved, after that sojer friend o' yours deserted ye? Amn't I after keepin' ye here two months, an' ye never had to go out once an' bring in any money same as any other girl. Eh? Ain't ye goin' to kiss me, Rosie?'

The woman never moved. He staggered against her and pressed his lips to her white cheek. She shuddered.

'Divil take ye. Yer like a dead thing. Is it how ye think I haven't got any money?' He fumbled at his shirt and pulled out a wad of bank-notes tied with a string. 'There's three hundred there. See? It takes the Wolf to get away with 'em. See? We're goin' to have a good time on them, Rosie. Me an' you, Rosie. See? Soon as these cops are off the hunt, we'll ship across t' England. See? They ain't goin' to get me. See?' He jumped to his feet, suddenly furious. 'Who's goin' to get me?' His voice came like a hiss between his teeth. Then he growled like a wild animal and stalked about the room with his gun levelled. 'See? I'm the Wolf Lanigan. The Wolf. D'ye hear?'

Suddenly he staggered and put his hand to his head.

'Blast it, my head is goin' round. Must have a sleep.' He moved over to the woman and whispered, 'Rosie, I'm goin' to lie down. See? You keep watch.'

He tumbled on to the bed and lay on his back with the pistol in his right hand across his chest. The woman's eyes were fixed on the fire. She sat immovable. The Wolf's eyes began to shut, but as soon as a noise came from outside, he started up and grabbed his pistol. Then gradually a weariness seized his limbs. They became listless. The weariness crept up into his head. His eyes shut. His mouth fell open. The hand slipped off the butt of the pistol. He began to snore. He was asleep.

Then slowly the woman turned her head around towards the bed and looked at him. Her eyes opened wide like the eyes of a child brought face to face with something strange and tremendous. Gradually a look of wonder spread over her face. Her lips were parted, showing her white teeth. She stood up with her hands down by her sides. The dressing-gown slipped from her shoulders. Mechanically she slipped her hands from the sleeves and let it fall to the ground. She stood in her nightdress, her hair plaited, white like an apparition. She walked over to the bed, moving straight and stiff. She stood over the bed looking down at the Wolf's face.

Then a strange, ghastly smile crept over her lips and cheeks without touching the eyes. The eyes became cold and glassy; two large disks lit with an immeasurable hatred, while her lips smiled. Her right hand moved forward slowly until it reached the pistol. Slowly the fingers crept around the butt. Then the smile faded from her lips. Her eyeballs started from the sockets. Her teeth bared. She drew in a deep breath, pressed the pistol to the Wolf's chest and pressed the trigger.

There was a deafening roar as bullet after bullet crashed through the sleeper's breast. Then in the silence that followed, the rattling of the window, the fragments of the lamp falling to the floor sounded like the dying echo of a thunder-clap. The woman turned, dropped the smoking pistol to the floor and burst into a wild shriek of insane laughter. Then there was silence again. Little clouds of smoke roamed about the ceiling. The figure on the bed was still.

THE BLACK BULLOCK

He was two years old when he came to Inverara. But he had been hungry all his life and he was no bigger than a donkey. His owner was a boatman on the mainland opposite Inverara and he had bought the black bullock for ten shillings when the bullock was a week old. Its mother had died of the colic or something (the poor widow who owned her said it was the Evil Eye). But the boatman had no land and the bullock grew up about the cabin, more accustomed to potato skins and nettles than to hay or clover or plain grass. By day he wandered around the little fishing hamlet, rambling on the roadside, chased by dogs and pelted by children, and by night he was tethered in his owner's kitchen to an iron hook in the wall by the back door. There was a deep groove around his neck where the rope rested, and the groove was deepest under his chin. For the lads of the village who visited his owner's cabin often amused themselves at night when the boatman was not looking by holding a potato in front of the bullock's mouth and retreating with it as the bullock strained after it moaning with hunger. Little boys amused themselves by riding him and sticking thistle heads in the end of his tail that only reached halfway down his legs. Yet he was by nature so healthy that his temper never soured under this ill-treatment and, in spite of hunger, his black hide was glossy and curly. He had no horns, and the tip of his skull where bullocks have horns was always caked with dried mud, for he was in the habit of playfully butting his head into the bog and wallowing like a wild one.

Then on the festival of the pagan god Crom Dugh in autumn his owner brought him to the island of Inverara to graze for the winter, in the hope that he would get fat, and be fit for sale in the following May. He gave him to a peasant named Jimmy Hernon of Coillnamhan. 'Feed him well, Jimmy', he said, 'and I'll bring you the best boatload of turf that was ever cut in a bog when I am taking him away next May Day.' Hernon took off his hat, spat on both hands and swore by all the saints that he would keep the bullock's belly full if his own had to go empty. In the presence of the boatman he put the little black bullock to graze in a clover field with his own cow. 'There you are', he said. 'There isn't a man in Inverara would treat your

94

bullock so well.' And the boatman went away to the mainland highly pleased with the bargain he had made.

As soon as the little black bullock found himself loose in the luscious clover he began to eat ravenously, wagging his tail, shaking his head and snorting. When he began to eat his belly was so thin that one could transfix it with a knitting needle, but it rapidly filled out so that he looked like a little cask. He soon made friends with the cow, although at first she horned him away when he sniffed at her flanks, and they wandered up and down the field all night side by side, their coarse tongues making a noise like tearing silk as they chopped the clover. Then in the morning when the cow leaned over the gap chewing her cud and lowed now and again wanting to be milked, the little black bullock stood by, chewing his cud with his eyes half shut, perfectly content.

But Hernon came with his wife to milk the cow and began to swear ferociously when he saw the black bullock's rotund stomach. 'I'll declare', he said with an oath, 'that he'll eat three times as much as my cow, the miserable little wretch. Out he goes to the crag this very minute.' And he drove the bullock from the clover field up a rocky lane to the cliff top, hammering him with a big stick, so that the bullock ran and stumbled and bellowed, wondering what was happening to him. Then Hernon put him to graze in a broad barren crag overlooking the sea and went away.

The bullock roamed about the crag for a long time, scarcely able to make his way over the jagged rocks and pointed loose stones. Several times he tried to nibble at the stunted grass that grew in the tiny valleys, but the grass tasted too salt and sour. And the sea roared near him. And the crag was so high and exposed that it caught every breeze and gust of wind, so that he felt very miserable and was struck with terror. For he had always been used to living among people and within sight of houses and shelter. All day he never ate anything, even of the stunted grass that grew there, but spent most of the time circling the crag trying to find a way out. The fence was not very high and he might easily jump it or knock it down by thrusting his breast against it, but his terror was so acute that he was unable to muster up courage to do so. When he passed along the brink of the cliff overlooking the sea, where there was no fence, he was continually snorting and jumping sideways with fright.

Then night came and he had nowhere to take shelter from the bitter autumn wind that rose from the sea. Next morning his hide was wet with dew and sea froth and his belly was as empty as it had been when he landed in Inverara. As day advanced the sun shone brightly, warming him, so he capered about nibbling and felt fairly comfortable, though his hoofs were sore from treading the sharp rocks. The best grass grew in the deep crevices in the rocks and he had to scramble over the most difficult ground to reach it, sometimes even going on his knees and straining his neck down into the holes. When he had eaten sufficient he wanted to drink, and that too was difficult, for the little pools were almost dry and it was only after visiting six of them, scattered at long intervals, that he was satisfied.

He spent a week that way without seeing a soul, and every day he became hungrier, more thirsty and miserable. Then three wandering goats came on to his crag and stayed the day prancing about the cliff top. He tried to make friends with them, but when he came near them and stretched out his head and sniffed, they stamped and snorted and ran away. And in the evening they departed eastwards, jumping a low part of the fence quite easily. He stood looking over the fence where they had leaped a long time, lowing after them until they disappeared. Then, seized with fury, he pushed against the fence, knocked off a few stones and scrambled through the gap in a heap to the other side.

With his tail in the air he ran along in the direction the goats had gone until he came to a lane. There he met a donkey with a young foal. He nestled up to the donkey, but the donkey kicked him in the belly and then bared her teeth and tried to bite him. So he wandered on, until he saw a village ahead of him.

When he saw the houses and the people he thought he was home again. He began to low with joy and, tossing his head, he trotted along snorting playfully. But straying round the village smelling at gates and dunghills he was chased by dogs, and peasant women ran out and threw stones at him, so that he retired miserably to a waste plot at the back of a barn and lay down, very weary of life. For these people regarded him as a wild beast and would not let him come near them.

Then two stray dogs discovered him and chased him down to the village cross-roads where a number of young men were loafing. The young men, bored for want of amusement, herded him into a corner and tied a tin kettle to his short tail. Then they beat him and shouted 'Fe-och, fe-och' and turned him out into the road again. The tin kettle just tipped the ground, and at every step the bullock took it clattered against his heels.

He began to trot in order to get away from it. But the more he trotted the greater was the noise it made and it hit his heels all the harder. Then he got mad, lashed out with his hind legs and broke into a gallop. The dogs barked and ran alongside him, biting at his mouth and his flanks. The men yelled and urged on the dogs. The bullock ran on and on frothing at the mouth until he reached a gap in the road fence that led into a crag. He rushed through the gap and on to the crag. But the kettle made a greater noise on the limestone crag and the dogs were better able to bite him, since he had to go slower. So he began to bellow and jumped headlong down into a little glen. It was but ten feet of a fall, but his hind hoof caught in a crevice as he jumped, and he fell on his back.

When Hernon found him his spine was broken, so he had to slaughter him.

GOING INTO EXILE

Patrick Feeney's cabin was crowded with people. In the large kitchen men, women and children lined the walls, three deep in places, sitting on forms, chairs, stools, and on one another's knees. On the cement floor three couples were dancing a jig and raising a quantity of dust, which was, however, soon sucked up the chimney by the huge turf fire that blazed on the hearth. The only clear space in the kitchen was the corner to the left of the fireplace, where Pat Mullaney sat on a yellow chair, with his right ankle resting on his left knee, a spotted red handkerchief on his head that reeked with perspiration, and his red face contorting as he played a tattered old accordian. One door was shut and the tins hanging on it gleamed in the firelight. The opposite door was open and over the heads of the small boys that crowded in it and outside it, peering in at the dancing couples in the kitchen, a starry June sky was visible and, beneath the sky, shadowy grey crags and misty, whitish fields lay motionless, still and sombre. There was a deep, calm silence outside the cabin and within the cabin, in spite of the music and dancing in the kitchen, a starry June sky was visible and, beneath the sky, Patrick Feeney's eldest son Michael sat on the bed with three other young men, there was a haunting melancholy in the air.

The people were dancing, laughing and singing with a certain forced and boisterous gaiety that failed to hide from them the real cause of their being there, dancing singing and laughing. For the dance was on account of Patrick Feeney's two children, Mary and Michael, who were going to the United States on the following morning.

Feeney himself, a black-bearded, red-faced, middle-aged peasant, with white ivory buttons on his blue frieze shirt and his hands stuck in his leather waist belt, wandered restlessly about the kitchen, urging the people to sing and dance, while his mind was in agony all the time, thinking that on the following day he would lose his two eldest children, never to see them again perhaps. He kept talking to everybody about amusing things, shouted at the dancers and behaved in a boisterous and abandoned manner. But every now and then he had to leave the kitchen, under the pretence of going to the pigsty to look at a

young pig that was supposed to be ill. He would stand, however, upright against his gable and look gloomily at some star or
other, while his mind struggled with vague and perculiar ideas
that wandered about in it. He could make nothing at all of his
thoughts, but a lump always came up his throat, and he
shivered, although the night was warm.

Then he would sigh and say with a contraction of his neck:
'Oh, it's a queer world this and no doubt about it. So it is.' Then
he would go back to the cabin again and begin to urge on the
dance, laughing, shouting and stamping on the floor.

Towards dawn, when the floor was crowded with couples,
arranged in fours, stamping on the floor and going to and fro,
dancing the 'Walls of Limerick', Feeney was going out to the
gable when his son Michael followed him out. The two of them
walked side by side about the yard over the grey sea pebbles
that had been strewn there the previous day. They walked in
silence and yawned without need, pretending to be taking the
air. But each of them was very excited, Michael was taller than
his father and not so thickly built, but the shabby blue serge
suit that he had bought for going to America was too narrow
for his broad shoulders and the coat was too wide around the
waist. He moved clumsily in it and his hands appeared altogether too bony and big and red, and he didn't know what to do
with them. During his twenty-one years of life he had never
worn anything other than the homespun clothes of Inverara,
and the shop-made clothes appeared as strange to him and as
uncomfortable as a dress suit worn by a man working in a
sewer. His face was flushed a bright red and his blue eyes shone
with excitement. Now and again he wiped the perspiration from
his forehead with the lining of his grey tweed cap.

At last Patrick Feeney reached his usual position at the gable
end. He halted, balanced himself on his heels with his hands in
his waist belt, coughed and said, 'It's going to be a warm day.'
The son came up beside him, folded his arms and leaned his
right shoulder against the gable.

'It was kind of Uncle Ned to lend the money for the dance,
father', he said. 'I'd hate to think that we'd have to go without
something or other, just the same as everybody else has. I'll
send you that money the very first money I earn, father . . .
even before I pay Aunt Mary for my passage money. I should
have all that money paid off in four months, and then I'll have
some more money to send you by Christmas.'

And Michael felt very strong and manly recounting what he
was going to do when he got to Boston, Massachusetts. He told
himself that with his great strength he would earn a great deal

99

of money. Conscious of his youth and his strength and lusting for adventurous life, for the moment he forgot the ache in his heart that the thought of leaving his father inspired in him.

The father was silent for some time. He was looking at the sky with his lower lip hanging, thinking of nothing. At last he sighed as a memory struck him. 'What is it?' said the son. 'Don't weaken, for God's sake. You will only make it hard for me.' 'Fooh!' said the father suddenly with pretended gruffness. 'Who is weakening? I'm afraid that your new clothes make you impudent.' Then he was silent for a moment and continued in a low voice: 'I was thinking of that potato field you sowed alone last spring the time I had influenza. I never set eyes on the man that could do it better. It's a cruel world that takes you away from the land that God made for you for.'

'Oh, what are you talking about, father?' said Michael irritably. 'Sure what did anybody ever get out of the land but poverty and hard work and potatoes and salt?'

'Ah yes', said the father with a sigh, 'but it's your own, the land, and over there' – he waved his hand at the western sky – you'll be giving your sweat to some other man's land, or what's equal to it.'

'Indeed', muttered Michael, looking at the ground with a melancholy expression in his eyes, 'it's poor encouragement you are giving me.'

They stood in silence fully five minutes. Each hungered to embrace the other, to cry, to beat the air, to scream with excess of sorrow. But they stood silent and sombre, like nature about them, hugging their woe. Then they went back to the cabin. Michael went into the little room to the left of the kitchen, to the three young men who fished in the same curragh with him and were his bosom friends. The father walked into the large bedroom to the right of the kitchen.

The large bedroom was also crowded with people. A large table was laid for tea in the centre of the room and about a dozen young men were sitting at it, drinking tea and eating buttered raisin cake. Mrs Feeney was bustling about the table, serving the food and urging them to eat. She was assisted by her two younger daughters and by another woman, a relative of her own. Her eldest daughter Mary, who was going to the United States that day, was sitting on the edge of the bed with several other young women. The bed was a large four poster bed with a deal canopy over it, painted red, and the young women were huddled together on it. So that there must have been about a dozen of them there. They were Mary Feeney's particular friends, and they stayed with her in that uncomfortable position just to show how much they liked her. It was a custom.

Mary herself sat on the edge of the bed with her legs dangling. She was a pretty, dark-haired girl of nineteen, with dimpled, plump, red cheeks and ruminative brown eyes that seemed to cause little wrinkles to come and go in her little low forehead. Her nose was soft and small and rounded. Her mouth was small and the lips were red and open. Beneath her white blouse that was frilled at the neck and her navy blue skirt that outlined her limbs as she sat on the edge of the bed, her body was plump, soft, well-moulded and in some manner exuded a feeling of freshness and innocence. So that she seemed to have been born to be fondled and admired in luxurious surroundings instead of having been born a peasant's daughter, who had to go to the United States that day to work as a servant or maybe in a factory.

And as she sat on the edge of the bed crushing her little handkerchief between her palms, she kept thinking feverishly of the United States, at one moment with fear and loathing, at the next with desire and longing. Unlike her brother she did not think of the work she was going to do or the money that she was going to earn. Other things troubled her, things of which she was half ashamed, half afraid, thoughts of love and of foreign men and of clothes and of houses where there were more than three rooms and where people ate meat every day. She was fond of life, and several young men among the local gentry had admired her in Inverara. But . . .

She happened to look up and she caught her father's eyes as he stood silently by the window with his hands stuck in his waist belt. His eyes rested on hers for a moment and then he dropped them without smiling, and with his lips compressed he walked down into the kitchen. She shuddered slightly. She was a little afraid of her father, although she knew that he loved her very much and he was very kind to her. But the winter before he had whipped her with a dried willow rod, when he caught her one evening behind Tim Hernon's cabin after nightfall, with Tim Hernon's son Bartly's arms around her waist and he kissing her. Ever since, she always shivered slightly when her father touched her or spoke to her.

'Oho!' said an old peasant who sat at the table with a saucer full of tea in his hand and his grey flannel shirt open at his thin, hairy, wrinkled neck. 'Oho! indeed, but it's a disgrace to the island of Inverara to let such a beautiful woman as your daughter go away, Mrs Feeney. If I were a young man, I'd be flayed alive if I'd let her go.'

There was a laugh and some of the women on the bed said: 'Bad cess to you, Patsy Coyne, if you haven't too much impudence, it's a caution.' But the laugh soon died. The young men sitting at the table felt embarrassed and kept looking at one another sheepishly, as if each tried to find out if the others were in love with Mary Feeney.

'Oh, well, God is good', said Mrs Feeney, as she wiped her lips with the tip of her bright, clean, check apron. 'What will be must be, and sure there is hope from the sea, but there is no hope from the grave. It is sad and the poor have to suffer, but ... ' Mrs Feeney stopped suddenly, aware that all these platitudes meant nothing whatsoever. Like her husband she was unable to think intelligently about her two children going away. Whenever the reality of their going away, maybe for ever, three thousand miles into a vast unknown world, came before her mind, it seemed that a thin bar of some hard metal thrust itself forward from her brain and rested behind the wall of her forehead. So that almost immediately she became stupidly conscious of the pain caused by the imaginary bar of metal and she forgot the dread prospect of her children going away. But her mind grappled with the things about her busily and efficiently, with the preparation of food, with the entertaining of her guests, with the numerous little things that have to be done in a house where there is a party and which only a woman can do properly. These little things, in a manner, saved her, for the moment at least, from bursting into tears whenever she looked at her daughter and whenever she thought of her son, whom she loved most of all her children, because perhaps she nearly died giving birth to him and he had been very delicate until he was twelve years old. So she laughed down in her breast a funny laugh she had that made her heave where her check apron rose out from the waist band in a deep curve. 'A person begins to talk', she said with a shrug of her shoulders sideways, 'and then a person says foolish things.'

'That's true', said the old peasant, noisily pouring more tea from his cup to his saucer.

But Mary knew by her mother laughing that way that she was very near being hysterical. She always laughed that way before she had one of her fits of hysterics. And Mary's heart stopped beating suddenly and then began again at an awful rate as her eyes became acutely conscious of her mother's body, the rotund, short body with the wonderful mass of fair hair growing grey at the temples and the fair face with the soft liquid brown eyes, that grew hard and piercing for a moment as they looked at a thing and then grew soft and liquid again, and the thin-lipped small mouth with the beautiful white teeth and the deep perpendicular grooves in the upper lip and the tremor that always came in the corner of the mouth, with love, when she looked at her children. Mary became acutely conscious of all these little points, as well as of the little black spot that was on her left breast below the nipple and the swelling than came now and again in her legs and caused her to have hysterics and would one day cause her death. And she was stricken with horror at the thought of leaving her mother and at the selfishness of her thoughts. She had never been prone to thinking of anything important but now, somehow for a moment, she had a glimpse of her mother's life that made her shiver and hate herself as a cruel, heartless, lazy, selfish wretch. Her mother's life loomed up before her eyes, a life of continual misery and suffering, hard work, birth pangs, sickness and again hard work and hunger and anxiety. It loomed up and then it fled again, a little mist came before her eyes and she jumped down from the bed, with the jaunty twirl of her head that was her habit when she set her body in motion.

'Sit down for a while, mother', she whispered, toying with one of the black ivory buttons on her mother's brown bodice. 'I'll look after the table.' 'No, no', murmured the mother with a shake of her whole body, 'I'm not a bit tired. Sit down, my treasure. You have a long way to travel to-day.'

And Mary sighed and went back to the bed again.

At last somebody said : 'It's broad daylight.' And immediately everybody looked out and said: 'So it is, and may God be praised.' The change from the starry night to the grey, sharp dawn was hard to notice until it had arrived. People looked out and saw the morning light sneaking over the crags silently, along the ground, pushing the mist banks upwards. The stars were growing dim. A long way off invisible sparrows were chirping in their ivied perch in some distant hill or other. Another day had arrived and even as the people looked at it, yawned and began to search for their hats, caps and shawls preparing to go home, the day grew and spread its light and made things move and give voice. Cocks crew, blackbirds carolled, a dog let loose from a cabin by an early riser chased madly after an imaginary robber, barking as if his tail were on fire. The people said goodbye and began to stream forth from Feeney's cabin. They were going to their homes to see to the morning's work before going to Kilmurrage to see the emigrants off on the steamer to the mainland. Soon the cabin was empty except for the family.

All the family gathered into the kitchen and stood about for some minutes talking sleepily of the dance and of the people who had been present. Mrs Feeney tried to persuade everybody to go to bed, but everybody refused. It was four o'clock and Michael and Mary would have to set out for Kilmurrage at nine. So tea was made and they all sat about for an hour drinking it and eating raisin cake and talking. They only talked of the dance and of the people who had been present.

There were eight of them there, the father and mother and six children. The youngest child was Thomas, a thin boy of twelve, whose lungs made a singing sound every time he breathed. The next was Bridget, a girl of fourteen, with dancing eyes and a habit of shaking her short golden curls every now and then for no apparent reason. Then there were the twins, Julia and Margaret, quiet, rather stupid, flat-faced girls of sixteen. Both their upper front teeth protruded slightly and they were both great workers and very obedient to their mother. They were all sitting at the table, having just finished a third large pot of tea, when suddenly the mother hastily gulped down the re-mainder of the tea in her cup, dropped the cup with a clatter to her saucer and sobbed once through her nose.

'Now mother', said Michael sternly, 'what's the good of this work?'

'No, you are right, my pulse', she replied quietly. 'Only I was just thinking how nice it is to sit here surrounded by all my children, all my little birds in my nest, and then two of them going to fly away made me sad.' And she laughed, pretending to treat it as a foolish joke.

'Oh, that be damned for a story', said the father, wiping his mouth on his sleeve; 'there's work to be done. You Julia, go and get the horse. Margaret, you milk the cow and see that you give enough milk to the calf this morning.' And he ordered everybody about as if it were an ordinary day of work.

But Michael and Mary had nothing to do and they sat about miserably conscious that they had cut adrift from the routine of their home life. They no longer had any place in it. In a few hours they would be homeless wanderers. Now that they were cut adrift from it, the poverty and sordidness of their home life appeared to them under the aspect of comfort and plenty.

So the morning passed until breakfast time at seven o'clock. The morning's work was finished and the family was gathered together again. The meal passed in a dead silence. Drowsy after the sleepless night and conscious that the parting would come in a few hours, nobody wanted to talk. Everybody had an egg for breakfast in honour of the occasion. Mrs Feeney, after her usual habit, tried to give her egg first to Michael, then to Mary, and as each refused it, she ate a little herself and gave the remainder to little Thomas who had the singing in his chest. Then the breakfast was cleared away. The father went to put the creels on the mare so as to take the luggage into Kilmurrage. Michael and Mary got the luggage ready and began to get dressed. The mother and the other children tidied up the house. People from the village began to come into the kitchen, as was customary, in order to accompany the emigrants from their home to Kilmurrage.

At last everything was ready. Mrs Feeney had exhausted all excuses for moving about, engaged on trivial tasks. She had to go into the big bedroom where Mary was putting on her new hat. The mother sat on a chair by the window, her face contorting on account of the flood of tears she was keeping back. Michael moved about the room uneasily, his two hands knotting a big red handkerchief behind his back. Mary twisted about in front of the mirror that hung over the black wooden mantlepiece. She was spending a long time with the hat. It was the first one she had ever worn, but it fitted her beautifully, and it was in excellent taste. It was given to her by the schoolmistress, who was very fond of her, and she herself had taken it in a little. She had an instinct for beauty in dress and deportment.

But the mother, looking at how well her daughter wore the cheap navy blue costume and the white frilled blouse, and the little round black hat with a fat, fluffy, glossy curl covering each ear, and the black silk stockings with blue clocks in them, and the little black shoes that had laces of three colours in them, got suddenly enraged with . . . She didn't know with what she got enraged. But for the moment she hated her daughter's beauty, and she remembered all the anguish of giving birth to her and nursing her and toiling for her, for no other purpose than to lose her now and let her go away, maybe to be ravished wantonly because of her beauty and her love of gaiety. A cloud of mad jealousy and hatred against this impersonal beauty that she saw in her daughter almost suffocated the mother, and she stretched out her hands in front of her unconsciously and then just as suddenly her anger vanished like a puff of smoke, and she burst into wild tears, wailing: 'My children, oh, my children, far over the sea you will be carried from me, your mother.' And she began to rock herself and she threw her apron over her head.

Immediately the cabin was full of the sound of bitter wailing. A dismal cry rose from the women gathered in the kitchen. 'Far over the sea they will be carried', began woman after woman, and they they all rocked themselves and hid their heads in their

105

aprons. Michael's mongrel dog began to howl on the hearth. Little Thomas sat down on the hearth beside the dog and, putting his arms around him, he began to cry, although he didn't know exactly why he was crying, but he felt melancholy on account of the dog howling and so many people being about.

In the bedroom the son and daughter, on their knees, clung to their mother, who held their heads between her hands and rained kisses on both heads ravenously. After the first wave of tears she had stopped weeping. The tears still ran down her cheeks, but her eyes gleamed and they were dry. There was a fierce look in them as she searched all over the heads of her two children with them, with her brows contracted, searching with a fierce terror-stricken expression, as if by the intensity of her stare she hoped to keep a living photograph of them before her mind. With her quivering lips she made a queer sound like 'im-m-m-m' and she kept kissing. Her right hand clutched at Mary's left shoulder and with her left she fondled the back of Michael's neck. The two children were sobbing freely. They must have stayed that way a quarter of an hour.

Then the father came into the room, dressed in his best clothes. He wore a new frieze waistcoat, with a grey and black front and a white back. He held his soft black felt hat in one hand and in the other hand he had a bottle of holy water. He coughed and said in a weak gentle voice that was strange to him, as he touched his son: 'Come now, it is time.'

Mary and Michael got to their feet. The father sprinkled them with holy water and they crossed themselves. Then, without looking at their mother, who lay in the chair with her hands clasped on her lap, looking at the ground in a silent tearless stupor, they left the room. Each hurriedly kissed little Thomas, who was not going to Kilmurrage, and then, hand in hand, they left the house. As Michael was going out the door he picked a piece of loose whitewash from the wall and put it in his pocket. The people filed out after them, down the yard and on to the road, like a funeral procession. The mother was left in the house with little Thomas and two old peasant women from the village. Nobody spoke in the cabin for a long time.

Then the mother rose and came into the kitchen. She looked at the two women, at her little son and at the hearth, as if she were looking for something she had lost. Then she threw her hands into the air and ran out into the yard.

'Come back', she screamed; 'come back to me.'

She looked wildly down the road with dilated nostrils, her bosom heaving. But there was nobody in sight. Nobody replied.

There was a crooked stretch of limestone road, surrounded by grey crags that were scorched by the sun. The road ended in a hill and then dropped out of sight. The hot June day was silent. Listening foolishly for an answering cry, the mother imagined she could hear the crags simmering under the hot rays of the sun. It was something in her head that was singing.

The two old women led her back into the kitchen. 'There is nothing that time will not cure', said one. 'Yes. Time and patience', said the other.

THE TENT

A sudden squall struck the tent. White glittering hailstones struck the shabby canvas with a wild noise. The tent shook and swayed slightly forward, dangling its tattered flaps. The pole creaked as it strained. A rent appeared near the top of the pole like a silver seam in the canvas. Water immediately trickled through the seam, making a dark blob.

A tinker and his two wives were sitting on a heap of straw in the tent, looking out through the entrance at the wild moor that stretched in front of it, with a snowcapped mountain peak rising like the tip of a cone over the ridge of the moor about two miles away. The three of them were smoking cigarettes in silence. It was evening, and they had pitched their tent for the night in a gravel pit on the side of the mountain road crossing from one glen to another. Their donkey was tethered to the cart beside the tent.

When the squall came the tinker sat up with a start and looked at the pole. He stared at the seam in the canvas for several moments and then he nudged the two women and pointed upwards with a jerk of his nose. The women looked but nobody spoke. After a minute or so the tinker sighed and struggled to his feet.

'I'll throw a few sacks over the top', he said.

He picked up two brown sacks from the heap of blankets and clothes that were drying beside the brazier in the entrance and went out. The women never spoke, but kept on smoking. The tinker kicked the donkey out of his way. The beast had stuck his hind quarters into the entrance of the tent as far as possible, in order to get the heat from the wood burning in the brazier. The donkey shrank away sideways still chewing a wisp of the hay which the tinker had stolen from a haggard the other side of the mountain. The tinker scrambled up the bank against which the tent was pitched. The bank was covered with rank grass into which yesterdays snow had melted in muddy cakes.

The top of the tent was only about eighteen inches above the bank. Beyond the bank there was a narrow rough road, with a thick copse of pine trees on the far side, within the wired fence of a demesne, but the force of the squall was so great that it swept through the trees and struck the top of the tent as violently as if it were standing exposed on the open moor. The tinker had to lean against the wind to prevent himself being carried away. He looked into the wind with wide-open nostrils.

'It can't last', he said, throwing the two sacks over the tent, where there was a rent in the canvas. He then took a big needle from his jacket and put a few stiches in them.

He was about to jump down from the bank when somebody hailed him from the road. He looked up and saw a man approaching, with his head thrust forward against the wind. The tinker scowled and shrugged his shoulders. He waited until the man came up to him.

The stranger was a tall, sturdily built man, with a long face and firm jaws and great sombre dark eyes, a fighter's face. When he reached the tinker he stood erect with his feet together and his hands by his sides like a soldier. He was fairly well dressed, his face was clean and well shaved, and his hands were clean. There was a blue figure of something or other tattooed on the back of his right hand. He looked at the tinker frankly with his sombre dark eyes. Neither spoke for several moments.

'Good evening', the stranger said.

The tinker nodded without speaking. He was looking the stranger up and down, as if he were slightly afraid of this big, sturdy man, who was almost like a policeman or a soldier or somebody in authority. He looked at the man's boots especially. In spite of the muck of the roads, the melted snow and the hailstones, they were still fairly clean, and looked as if they were constantly polished.

'Travellin'?' he said at length.

'Eh', said the stranger, almost aggressively. 'Oh! Yes, I'm lookin' for somewhere to shelter for the night.'

The stranger glanced at the tent slowly and then looked back to the tinker again.

'Goin' far?' said the tinker.

'Don't know', said the stranger angrily. Then he almost shouted: 'I have no bloody place to go to . . . only the bloody roads.'

'All right, brother', said the tinker, 'come on.'

He nodded towards the tent and jumped down into the pit. The stranger followed him, stepping carefully down to avoid soiling his clothes.

When he entered the tent after the tinker and saw the women he immediately took off his cap and said: 'Good evening.' The two women took their cigarettes from their mouths, smiled and nodded their heads.

The stranger looked about him cautiously and then sat down on a box to the side of the door near the brazier. He put his hands to the blaze and rubbed them. Almost immediately a slight steam rose from his clothes. The tinker handed him a cigarette, murmuring: 'Smoke?'

The stranger accepted the cigarette, lit it, and then looked at them. None of them were looking at him, so he 'sized them up' carefully, looking at each suspiciously with his sombre dark eyes. The tinker was sitting on a box opposite him, leaning languidly backwards from his hips, a slim, tall, graceful man, with a beautiful head poised gracefully on a brown neck, and great black lashes falling down over his half-closed eyes, just like a woman. A womanish-looking fellow, with that sensuous grace in the languid pose of his body which is found only among aristocrats and people who belong to a very small work-less class, cut off from the mass of society, yet living at their expense. A young fellow with proud, contemptuous, closed lips and an arrogant expression in his slightly expanded nostrils. A silent fellow, blowing out cigarette smoke through his nostrils and gazing dreamily into the blaze of the wood fire. The two women were just like him in texture, both of them slatterns, dirty and unkempt, but with the same proud, arrogant, contemptuous look in their beautiful brown faces. One was dark-haired and black-eyed. She had a rather hard expression in her face and seemed very alert. The other woman was golden-haired, with a very small head and finely-developed jaw, that stuck out level with her forehead. She was surpassingly beautiful, in spite of her ragged clothes and the foul condition of her hair, which was piled on her tiny skull in knotted heaps, uncombed. The perfect symmetry and delicacy of her limbs, her bust and her long throat that had tiny freckles in the white skin, made the stranger feel afraid of her, of her beauty and her presence in the tent.

'Tinkers', he said to himself. 'Awful bloody people.'

Then he turned to the tinker.

'Got any grub in the place...eh...mate?' he said brusquely, his thick lips rapping out every word firmly, like one accustomed to command inferiors. He hesitated before he added the word 'mate', obviously disinclined to put himself on a level of human intercourse with the tinker.

The tinker nodded and turned to the dark-haired woman.

'Might as well have supper now, Kitty', he said softly.

The dark-haired woman rose immediately, and taking a blackened can that was full of water, she put it on the brazier. The stranger watched her. Then he addressed the tinker again.

'This is a hell of a way to be, eh?' he said. 'Stuck out on a mountain. Thought I'd make Roundwood to-night. How many miles is it from here?'

'Ten', said the tinker.

'Good God!' said the stranger.

Then he laughed, and putting his hand in his breast pocket, he pulled out a half-pint bottle of whiskey.

'That is all I got left', he said, looking at the bottle.

The tinker immediately opened his eyes wide when he saw the bottle. The golden-haired woman sat up and looked at the stranger eagerly, opening her brown eyes wide and rolling her tongue in her cheek. The dark-haired woman, rummaging in a box, also turned around to look. The stranger winked an eye and smiled.

'Always welcome', he said. 'Eh? My curse on it, anyway. Anybody got a corkscrew?'

The tinker took a knife from his pocket, pulled out a cork-screw from its side and handed it to the man. The man opened the bottle.

'Here', he said, handing the bottle to the tinker. 'Pass it round. I suppose the women'll have a drop.'

The tinker took the bottle and whispered to the dark-haired woman. She began to pass him mugs from the box.

'Funny thing', said the stranger, 'when a man is broke and hungry, he can get whiskey but he can't get grub. Met a man this morning in Dublin and he knew bloody well I was broke, but instead of asking me to have a meal, or giving me some money, he gave me that. I had it with me all along the road and I never opened it.'

He threw the end of his cigarette out the entrance.

'Been drinkin' for three weeks, curse it', he said.

'Are ye belonging to these parts?' murmured the tinker, pouring out the whiskey into the tin mugs.

'What's that?' said the man, again speaking angrily, as if he resented the question. Then he added: 'No. Never been here in me life before. Question of goin' into the workhouse or takin' to the roads. Got a job in Dublin yesterday. The men downed tools when they found I wasn't a member of the union. Thanks. Here's luck.'

'Good health, sir', the women said.

The tinker nodded his head only, as he put his own mug to his lips and tasted it. The stranger drained his at a gulp.

'Ha', he said. 'Drink up, girls. It's good stuff.'

He winked at them. They smiled and sipped their whiskey.

'My name is Carney', said the stranger to the tinker. 'What do they call you?'

'Byrne', said the tinker. 'Joe Byrne.'

'Hm! Byrne', said Carney. 'Wicklow's full o' Byrnes. Tinker, I suppose?'

'Yes', murmured the tinker, blowing a cloud of cigarette smoke through his puckered lips. Carney shrugged his shoulders.

'Might as well', he said. 'One thing is as good as another. Look at me. Sergeant-major in the army two months ago. Now I'm tramping the roads. That's boiling.'

The dark-haired woman took the can off the fire. The other woman tossed off the remains of her whiskey and got to her feet to help with the meal. Carney shifted his box back farther out of the way and watched the golden-haired woman eagerly. When she moved about her figure was so tall that she had to stoop low in order to avoid the roof of the tent. She must have been six feet in height, and she wore high-heeled shoes which made her look taller.

'There is a woman for ye', thought Carney. 'Must be a gentleman's daughter. Lots o' these shots out of a gun in the county Wicklow. Half the population is illegitimate. Awful moody people, these tinkers. I suppose the two of them belong to this Joe. More like a woman than a man. Suppose he never did a stroke of work in his life.'

There was cold rabbit for supper, with tea and bread and butter. It was excellent tea, and it tasted all the sweeter on account of the storm outside which was still raging. Sitting around the brazier they could see the hailstones driving through a grey mist, sweeping the bleak black moor, and the cone-shaped peak of the mountain in the distance, with a whirling cloud of snow around it. The sky was rent here and there with a blue patch, showing through the blackness.

They ate the meal in silence. Then the women cleared it away. They didn't wash the mugs or plates, but put everything away probably until morning. They sat down again after drawing out the straw, bed-shape, and putting the clothes on it that had been drying near the brazier. They all seemed to be in a good humour now with the whiskey and the food. Even the tinker's face had grown soft, and he kept puckering up his lips in a smile. He passed around cigarettes.

'Might as well finish that bottle', said Carney. 'Bother the mugs. We can drink outa the neck.'

'Tastes sweeter that way', said the golden-haired woman, laughing thickly, as if she were slightly drunk. At the same time she looked at Carney with her lips open.

Carney winked at her. The tinker noticed the wink and the girl's smile. His face clouded and closed his lips very tightly. Carney took a deep draught and passed him the bottle. The tinker nodded his head, took the bottle and put it to his lips.

'I'll have a stretch', said Carney. 'I'm done in. Twenty miles since morning. Eh?'

He threw himself down on the clothes beside the yellow-haired woman. She smiled and looked at the tinker. The tinker paused with the bottle to his lips and looked at her through almost closed eyes savagely. He took the bottle from his lips and bared his white teeth. The golden-headed woman shrugged her shoulders and pouted. The dark-haired woman laughed aloud, stretched back with one arm under her head and the other stretched out towards the tinker.

'Sht', she whistled through her teeth. 'Pass it along Joe.'

He handed her the bottle slowly, and as he gave it to her she clutched his hand and tried to pull him to her. But he tore his hand away, got up and walked out of the tent rapidly.

Carney had noticed nothing of this. He was lying close to the woman by his side. He could feel the softness of her beautiful body and the slight undulation of her soft side as she breathed. He became overpowered with desire for her and closed his eyes, as if to shut out the consciousness of the world and of the other people in the tent. Reaching down he seized her hand and pressed it. She answered the pressure. At the same time she turned to her companion and whispered:

'Where's he gone?'

'I dunno. Ran out.'

'What about?'

'Phst.'

'Give us a drop.'

'Here ye are.'

Carney heard the whispering, but he took no notice of it. He heard the golden-headed one drinking and then drawing a deep breath.

'Finished', she said. throwing the bottle to the floor. Then she laughed softly.

'I'm going out to see where he's gone', whispered the dark-haired one. She rose and passed out of the tent. Carney immediately turned around and tried to embrace the woman by his side. But she bared her teeth in a savage grin and pinioned his arms with a single movement.

'Didn't think I was strong', she said, putting her face close to his and grinning at him.

He looked at her seriously, surprised and still more excited.

'What ye goin' to do in Roundwood?' she said.

'Lookin' for a job', he muttered thickly.

She smiled and rolled her tongue in her cheek.

113

'Stay here', she said.

He licked his lip and winked his right eye. 'With you?'

She nodded.

'What about him?' he said, nodding towards the door.

She laughed silently. 'Are ye afraid of Joe?'

He did not reply, but, making a sudden movement, he seized her around the body and pressed her to him. She did not resist, but began to laugh, and bared her teeth as she laughed. He tried to kiss her mouth but she threw back her head and he kissed her cheek several times.

Then suddenly there was a hissing noise at the door. Carney sat up with a start. The tinker was standing in the entrance, stooping low, with his mouth open and his jaw twisted to the right, his two hands hanging loosely by his sides, with the fingers twitching. The dark-haired woman was standing behind him, peering over his shoulder. She was smiling.

Carney got to his feet, took a pace forward, and squared himself. He did not speak. The golden-headed woman uttered a loud peal of laughter, and, stretching out her arms, she lay flat on the bed, giggling.

'Come out here', hissed the tinker.

He stepped back. Carney shouted and rushed at him jumping the brazier. The tinker stepped aside and struck Carney a terrible blow in the jaw as he passed him. Carney staggered against the bank and fell in a heap. The tinker jumped on him like a cat, striking him with his hands and feet all together. Carney roared; 'Let me up, let me up. Fair play.' But the tinker kept on beating him until at last he lay motionless at the bottom of the pit.

'Ha', said the tinker.

Then he picked up the prone body, as lightly as if it were an empty sack, and threw it to the top of the bank. 'Be off, you – ' he hissed.

Carney struggled to his feet on the top of the bank and looked at the three of them. They were all standing now in front of the tent, the two women grinning, the tinker scowling. Then he staggered on to the road, with his hands to his head.

'Good-bye dearie', cried the golden-headed one.

Then she screamed. Carney looked behind and saw the tinker carrying her into the tent in his arms.

'God Almighty!' cried Carney, crossing himself.

Then he trudged away fearfully through the storm towards Roundwood.

'God Almighty!' he cried at every two yards. 'God Almighty!'

114

MILKING TIME

Softly, softly, the milk flowed from the taut tapering teats into its own white upward-heaving froth. It flowed from the two front teats, two white columns shooting, crossing and descending with a soft swirling movement through the billowing froth. There is no soft cadence as soothing as its sound, no scent as pure as its warm smell, cow smell, milk smell, blood smell, mingling with the thousand soft smells of a summer evening.

The cow stood on the summit of a grassy knoll. Behind her there was a rock-strewn ridge, making a grey horizon against the sky. In front there was a vast expanse of falling land, falling in flat terraces to the distant sea. Close by, the land was green-bright under the rays of the setting sun, but in the distance it was covered with a white mist, as if it rolled, dust-raising, to the sea.

The cow chewed her cud, looking through half-closed luminous eyes downwards at the mist-covered land, her red flanks shivering with content, the wanton pleasure of being milked by a sweet-smelling, crooning woman, the gentle pressure of the woman's fingers against her teats, softer than a calf's gums.

And the woman milking was in an ecstasy of happiness; for it was her first time milking her husband's cow; her cow now. They had been married on Thursday. It was now Sunday evening and they had come together to milk, as was the custom among the people.

He lay on the grass watching her milk, listening to her crooning voice and the voice of the birds; thinking.

'Isn't it wonderful how your little fingers can milk so quickly?' he said.

She turned her head and shook her towering mass of black hair proudly; smooth-combed, winding tresses of black hair gleaming in the twilight, red lips smiling as they crooned; full white throat swelling with soft words; crooning meaningless words of joy, as she looked at him.

He looked at her joyously and smiled, swallowing his breath.

'Wasn't it lovely to-day, Kitty', he murmured, 'coming from Mass?'

She bowed her head, crooning dreamily.

'Everybody was looking at us, as we came out of the chapel together. We are the tallest couple in the whole parish, and I heard several people talking about us in whispers as we passed along the road between the men sitting on the stone walls. Were you shy?'

'I was. I put my shawl out over my face, so they couldn't see me. I thought I'd never get out of sight of the people.'

'After all, it's a great thing', he said.

'What's a great thing, Michael?' His freckled face became serious. He looked away into the distance over the mist-covered falling land to where the dim horizon of the sea dwindled into a pale emptiness.

'How tall he is', she thought, 'and though his arms are hard like iron, he touches me gently.'

'What's a great thing, Michael?' she said again.

'Well! It's hard to say what it is, but we are here now together and there's nothing else, is there?'

'How?'

'Before, on a Sunday evening I always wanted to wander off somewhere a long way and maybe get drunk, but now I don't want anything at all only just to lie here and watch you milking the cow.'

She did not reply. She flushed slightly and bent her head against the cow's warm side, thinking of other Sundays when she sat among the village women on the green hill above the beach, singing songs as they knitted. Then she too longed for something shyly, awakening, nameless longings for a gentle strong voice and the gentle pressure of strong arms.

'But', she said, 'men are queer', and changing her hands she drew at the two hind teats, wetting them first with froth and pulling slowly until two fresh white streams flowed downward.

The cow raised a hoof languidly and stamped, swinging her tail. Michael laughed.

'Maybe they are', he said.

'Michael!'

'What?'

'Sure you won't be going off again on Sunday evenings to get drunk after you get tired of me?'

'I'll never get tired of you, Kitty.'

'Ah, yes, it's easy saying that now when we are only a few days married, but maybe . . .'

'No, Kitty, there's going to be no maybe with us. We'll have too much work to do to get tired of one another. It's only people who have nothing to do that get tired of one another.'

'It will be lovely working together, Michael. I love pulling

116

potato stalks in autumn and then picking the potatoes off the ridge, and at dinner-time we'll roast a few in the ground with a fire of stalks.'

'The two of us.'

'Yes.'

'But we have all summer before that. There isn't much work in summer, only fishing. I'm going fishing to-morrow.'

'Then you'll be away all day and I'll be so lonely with nobody in the house.'

'You won't feel it until I'll come back in the evening with a whole lot of fish. It would be grand to take you with me in the boat, but people would be laughing at us.'

'Won't it be grand if you get fish? I love to spill them out of a basket on a flag and see them slipping about. And they'll be my fish now. You'll catch them for me. Oh! It is grand, Michael.'

They became silent as she finished milking, passing from teat to teat, drawing the dregs, the richest of the milk. It was like a ceremony, this first milking together, initiating them into the mysterious glamour of mating; and both their minds were awed at the new strange knowledge that had come to their simple natures, something that belonged to them both, making their souls conscious of their present happiness with a dim realization of the great struggle that would follow it, struggling with the earth and with the sea for food. And this dim realization tinged their happiness with a gentle sadness, without which happiness is ever coarse and vulgar.

She finished milking, Michael rose and split half the milk into a bucket for the calf.

'You take it to him', he said, 'so that he'll get used to you.'

The cow lowed lazily, looking at them with great eyes; she walked with heavy hoofs to the fence beyond which her calf was waiting in a little field for his milk. Putting her head over the fence, she licked his upraised snout.

They pushed aside the cow's head and lowered the bucket to the calf. He dashed at it, sank his nozzle into the froth and began to drink greedily, his red curly back trembling with eagerness.

Kitty rubbed his forehead as he drank.

Then they walked home silently hand in hand, in the twilight.

THE CONGER EEL

He was eight feet long. At the centre of his back he was two feet in circumference. Slipping sinuously along the bottom of the sea at a gigantic pace, his black, mysterious body glistened and twirled like a wisp in a foaming cataract. His little eyes, stationed wide apart in his flat-boned, broad skull, searched the ocean for food. He coursed ravenously for miles along the base of the range of cliffs. He searched fruitlessly, except for three baby pollocks which he swallowed in one mouthful without arresting his progress. He was very hungry.

Then he turned by a sharp promontory and entered a cliff-bound harbour where the sea was dark and silent, shaded by the concave cliffs. Savagely he looked ahead into the dark waters. Then instantaneously he flicked his tail, rippling his body like a twisted screw, and shot forward. His long, thin, single whisker, hanging from his lower snout like a label tag, jerked back under his belly. His glassy eyes rested ferociously on minute white spots that scurried about in the sea a long distance ahead. The conger eel had sighted his prey. There was a school of mackerel a mile away.

He came upon them headlong, in a flash. He rose out of the deep from beneath their white bellies, and gripped one mackerel in his wide-open jaws ere his snout met the surface. Then, as if in a swoon, his body went limp, and tumbling over and over, convulsing like a crushed worm, he sank lower and lower until at last he had swallowed the fish. Then immediately he straightened out and flicked his tail, ready to pursue his prey afresh.

The school of mackerel, when the dread monster had appeared among them, were swimming just beneath the surface of the sea. When the eel rushed up they had hurled themselves clean out of the water with the sound of innumerable grains of sand being shaken in an immense sieve. The thousand blue and white bodies flashed and shimmered in the sun for three moments, and then they disappeared, leaving a large patch of the dark water convulsing turbulently. Ten thousand little fins cut the surface of the sea as the mackerel set off in headlong flight. Their white bellies were no longer visible. They plunged down into the depths of the sea, where their blue-black sides and backs, the colour of the sea, hid them from their enemy. The eel surged about in immense figures of eight; but he had lost them.

Half hungry, half satisfied, he roamed about for half an hour, a demented giant of the deep, travelling restlessly at an incredible speed. Then at last his little eyes again sighted his prey. Little white spots again hung like faded drops of brine in the sea ahead of him. He rushed thither. He opened his jaws as the spots assumed shape, and they loomed up close to his eyes. But just as he attempted to gobble the nearest one, he felt a savage impact. Then something hard and yet intangible pressed against his head and then down along his back. He leaped and turned somersault. The hard, gripping material completely enveloped him. He was in a net. While on all sides of him mackerel wriggled gasping in the meshes.

The eel paused for two seconds amazed and terrified. Then all around him he saw a web of black strands hanging miraculously in the water, everywhere, while mackerel with heaving gills stood rigid in the web, some with their tails and heads both caught and their bodies curved in an arch, others encompassed many times in the uneven folds, others girdled firmly below the gills with a single black thread. Glittering, they eddied back and forth with the stream of the sea, a mass of fish being strangled in the deep.

Then the eel began to struggle fiercely to escape. He hurtled hither and thither, swinging his long slippery body backwards and forwards, ripping with his snout, surging forward suddenly at full speed, churning the water. He ripped and tore the net, cutting great long gashes in it. But the more he cut and ripped the more deeply enmeshed did he become. He did not release himself, but he released some of the mackerel. They fell from the torn meshes, stiff and crippled, downwards, sinking like dead things. Then suddenly one after another they seemed to wake from sleep, shook their tails, and darted away, while the giant eel was gathering coil upon coil of the net about his slippery body. Then, at last, exhausted and half strangled, he lay still, heaving.

Presently he felt himself being hauled up in the net. The net crowded around him more, so that the little gleaming mackerel, imprisoned with him, rubbed his sides and lay soft and flabby against him, all hauled up in the net with him. He lay still, He reached the surface and gasped, but he made no movement. Then he was hauled heavily into a boat, and fell with a thud into the bottom.

The two fishermen in the boat began to curse violently when

they saw the monstrous eel that had torn their net and ruined their catch of mackerel. The old man on the oars in the bow called out: 'Free him and kill him, the whore.' The young man who was hauling in the net looked in terror at the slippery monster that lay between his feet, with its little eyes looking up cunningly, as if it were human. He almost trembled as he picked up the net and began to undo the coils. 'Slash it with your knife', yelled the old man, 'before he does more harm.' The young man picked up his knife from the gunwale where it was stuck, and cut the net, freeing the eel. The eel with a sudden and amazing movement, glided up the bottom of the boat, so that he stretched full length.

Then he doubled back, rocking the boat as he beat the sides with his whirling tail, his belly flopping in the water that lay in the bottom. The two men screamed, both crying: 'Kill him, or he'll drown us.' 'Strike him on the nable.' They both reached for the short, thick stick that hung from a peg amidships. The young man grabbed it, bent down, and struck at the eel. 'Hit him on the nable!' cried the old man; 'catch him, catch him, and turn him over.'

They both bent down, pawing at the eel, cursing and panting, while the boat rocked ominously and the huge conger eel glided around and around at an amazing speed. Their hands clawed his sides, slipping over them like skates on ice. They gripped him with their knees, they stood on him, they tried to lie on him, but in their confusion they could not catch him.

Then at last the young man lifted him in his arms, holding him in the middle, gripping him as if he were trying to crush him to death. He staggered upwards. 'Now strike him on the nable!' he yelled to the old man. But suddenly he staggered backwards. The boat rocked. He dropped the eel with an oath, reaching out with his hands to steady himself. The eel's head fell over the canted gunwale. His snout dipped into the sea. With an immense shiver, he glided away, straight down, down to the depths, down like an arrow, until he reached the dark, weed-covered rocks at the bottom.

Then stretching out to his full length he coursed in a wide arc to his enormous lair, far away in the silent depths.

CIVIL WAR

Day had dawned. It was the fourth day. Now everything was lost, but they would not surrender. They had crawled on to the roof and they waited for the soldiers to come as soon as it was light. They would be here shortly now. In the distance there was heavy machine-gun fire, and the sky was red in one quarter, not with the dull blaze of the rising summer sun, but with the dark red flare of flames mixed with black smoke, crackling upwards, winding and jumping in ghastly shapes, while timbers fell with monstrous jumbling sounds into the broad street, away to the right; where the Republican headquarters was surrounded and on the point of capture.

Here on the roof of a public-house, in a narrow slum street, the two men waited, waited for death. It was terrible.

Four days. How different everything was now. There, round about, stretching away on all sides from the black dusty roof, the multitudinous roofs of the city lay like an uneven plain, silent; a great roof covering a multitude of people that slept. They slept, snoring now in peace because everything was over, the end was in sight and the Republicans were defeated. Four days and the whole surging throng of Republicans, rushing with mad eagerness in their eyes to their posts, were all scattered, jailed, killed, wounded, hiding in the hills.

The two men crouched on the roof, with their pistols in their hands, waiting for the soldiers to come. One of them was Lieutenant Jim Dolan, a slim young man of twenty-two, with his new blue suit, that he had bought specially for the rising, all torn and covered with dirt, his white young face haggard and blotched with terror of death and with want of sleep, a clerk. The other was Quartermaster Tim Murphy, an enormous low-sized workman, with a neck like a bull and a great brown face ending in a square red jaw that stuck out like a broad upward-curving claw; little grey eyes hidden in pouched dark flesh and a snub nose; a resolute fanatical gunman; senseless, indomitable.

Murphy lay flat on his stomach with his chest resting against the low gutter of the roof, his head jammed against the chimney stack that rose erect from the corner of the roof, his pistol gripped loosely in his right hand close to his right eye, staring in front of him, waiting with desperate hatred for the first head to show. Thirty rounds left. Then death. All was lost now. There was no further need to live. Death. . . .

Dolan knelt on his right knee, with his buttock on his heel, also grasping his revolver. But the muzzle pointed at the gutter and his teeth chattered. He didn't want to die. The same hatred throbbed in his brain; hatred of the people who slept; hatred of the soldiers who were setting the distant street on fire and would come creeping through the houses towards him when the daylight spread. But he didn't want to die. The fear of death made his teeth chatter.

Thinking feverishly . . . he thought of the two corpses on the stairway, his two comrades that had been killed the day before when a passing lorry full of soldiers hurled a bomb. It burst with a deafening crash on the stairs. There were screams. The garrison went into panic. Three men bolted into the street, with their hands up, and surrendered. He, too, wanted to surrender. But Murphy was by his side at the top-floor window. Murphy fired, once, twice, three times. The three men twirled round and fell in the street. He fired again. Somebody screamed in the lorry and as it whirled away at full speed, a green-clothed body vaulted with curved spine in the middle of it and then fell among the crouching backs of the soldiers, who had fallen prone for shelter.

Now they were alone, the two of them. He was alone with Murphy and he feared him. He was in command, in charge of the post. But this bull-necked fiend was the real commander. There was no command now. They were alone. And Murphy was a devil.

Murphy had turned on him, stuck his pistol into his chest and roared, frothing, into his face: 'You bloody well stay with me. D'ye hear, you bastard? I'm in command and it's no surrender.'

That was yesterday evening. What a night! Silence, shots at a distance, rats on the stairs, thinking about his wife, Murphy prowling about muttering, two drunken men trying to enter the bar for loot, shots, curses, a scramble on to the roof just an hour ago and now . . . waiting for death. No surrender.

Dolan thought of his wife. God! How strange everything was. Was it four days or was it a thousand years? He did not love her now. Not at all. She had disappeared out of his life. There remained only memories of her thin frail hands, her delicate pink cheeks, the fair curls in bunches about her ears, her big pale blue eyes, and the absolute impossibility of making her understand anything. He hadn't told her anything. He didn't even send a message, when he rushed out of his office four days ago to take charge of his post. She wouldn't understand . . . anything. He only thought of her, because she represented the world as compared to this wilderness, where he was cut off completely from life, on a roof with a devil.

Why, why could he not scream for help? Why could he not turn his loaded revolver on the broad back of Murphy lying prone beside him and fire, fire, fire with clenched teeth and staring eyes, ferociously, until six bullets had entered the devilish body? Then he would be free. He could rush down the stairs past the . . . No. He could not pass the corpses. God! The corpses on the stairs!

With his teeth chattering he knelt, with a terrible pain in his head and his whole body on fire, every nerve throbbing, his bowels heavy as if they were made of lead and sagging down, so that every moment, he seemed to be on the point of going into a frenzied fit, during which, he thought, he would wander away for ever through an endless abyss peopled with devils who fired and screamed and cursed, endlessly.

Murphy never moved. His prone body was stiff, with the flesh lying loosely on the rigid bones, like a waiting animal at bay. Light spread, whitening, sparkling, warming the roof. Sounds approached.

At first came the rumble of rubbered wheels and the dull thumping of a motor. Then the rumbling sound stopped with a thud and there was a clatter of feet. Murphy grunted, shifted his elbows and stretched his heels out wide. Turning his head around slowly, he stared at Dolan. His eyes were bloodshot and almost closed.

'They're coming', he said. 'Good-bye. See ye in hell.'

The puffed flesh on his cheeks trembled as he laughed silently without opening his mouth. Then he stared for a few more moments at Dolan and turned to his front, grinding his teeth and levelling his Mauser pistol slowly towards the sounds.

Dolan also went rigid. His jaws set. His eyes opened wide, staring senselessly without seeing anything. He stopped thinking. His whole body waited. What?

Trup, trap, trip. They came. They were still invisible. The narrow street curved a hundred yards to the left. They would come around that corner, past a blank wall that faced an inward-curving, black-painted shop front, with J. WALSH, GROCER, painted on it in white letters, brown horse-dung dried on the narrow street, and a blank wall. Dolan stared at them, first one, then the other, senselessly.

Suddenly two green-clothed men appeared, walking slowly on either side of the street, their rifles at the high port, their caps set rakishly on the sides of their heads, one man chewing a long wisp of white straw, both staring upwards at the windows of the houses. They halted, spoke to another and then one looked behind and twirled his right hand above his head. He paused with his hand raised and then shot it forward and brought it stiffly to his side. Signal. Advance. They marched on. Two more men appeared. Then three more, all marching slowly with their rifles at the high port.

Murphy growled and then his body heaved as he gurgled his laughter silently. They were walking into his trap. He was waiting until they came beneath him, at close range. Then he would fire. . . .

But Dolan. . . . As soon as he saw them, his heart began to beat violently and his brain again began to work. He had no fear of them. He had forgotten that they were enemies, that he had been fighting them for four days. He had ceased to be a revolutionary. He was a prisoner, he thought, at the mercy of a murderer and madman, and here was hope of delivery. He tried to cry out to them and wave his hands, but somehow, the terrible power of the man beside him clove his tongue to the roof of his mouth and rendered his hands lifeless. He could only shiver and made inarticulate movements with his pallid lips.

They came closer. He could see the buttons on their tunics glimmering and the curious casual expression on their faces, as if they were strolling along carelessly. God! Why could they not know that he was here, in danger of death? Why were they coming like that so carelessly when . . . Hell!

Murphy moved. His right arm stiffened. The squat muzzle of his gun jutted downwards sharply. He was going to fire. Dolan screamed and threw himself on the prone body. With a growl Murphy whirled around, dashing his elbow backwards into Dolan's ribs. Dolan's light frame was hurled backwards with a slithering sound on to the slates of the roof. He fell on his back and slipped sideways into the gutter, with his face upwards, the head bent forward and the eyes staring at Murphy's. Murphy pointed his gun at Dolan's face. 'Ha', he said. Then there was a sharp crack. Dolan thought he was dead. But it was Murphy that was hit. His mouth opened wide and he fell backwards for a moment and then turned himself, twisting his body curiously all on the right side. His left side was helpless. There was a bullet in the upper part of his chest beneath the left shoulder. They had fired from the street.

Dolan threw back his head and lay flat. He still thought he was dead. His brain was whirling round and round at an amazing speed. There were revolving red circles before his closed eyes, and the extremities of his limbs seemed to be firmly bound with enormous weights that were dragging him downwards ever so slowly and yet leaving his body on the roof. He waited in terrible silence, hearing nothing.

As soon as the soldiers had fired they ran, taking shelter in a lane, a little way up the street on the lefthand side. Murphy had fired blindly, two rounds, but he had hit nobody. The bullets spattered against the edge of the black-fronted shop, making little dull white spots, side by side. Then he waited.

Suddenly there was another crack and Murphy's body shivered. His head bent backwards and he put his right hand to his throat. He was hit again, in the left shoulder near the neck. Immediately blood spurted out through his blue sweater. His mouth opened, his tongue came out and then his lips closed, gripping the end of his tongue. He closed his left eye, and with an immense effort levelled his gun at a chimney. Silence. Crack, crack, crack. He fired three times, rapidly. There was a yell and a man threw up his hands, curving inwards, with a rifle held slantwise in them. Then he fell forward and lay stretched across the chimney, writhing. Another figure jumped up and tried to drag him off, stooping low. Murphy fired again. The other figure fell back. Was he hit;

Dr-r-r-r-r. A Lewis gun spattered farther up. A whizzing stream of bullets passed in front of Murphy's face, moving from side to side in the air, as they whizzed, hot near his face. He ducked and lay still. Crack, crack, dr-r-r-r-r, crack. They were all at him, firing from all sides. Pieces of brick from the chimney stack and slivers of the slates from the roof pattered on his back. Still he was unhit, waiting in the gutter.

Waiting, he thought of Dolan. He would finish him off now, the traitor. He felt himself getting very weak. Only one side of him was alive. Death was coming rapidly. He would get that bastard though. Slowly he turned his head, brushing his skull against the low wall of the gutter, so as not to raise it against the background of the slates, on which the bullets were pattering. Then he had to bring his right arm around under his elbow and move his right knee up under his hip. He was a long time shuffling and groaning with the terrible pain of his wounds.

Dolan heard him move and started with terror. This movement brought him back to consciousness again, like a man waking suddenly from a nightmare on hearing a noise in his room. He thrust forward his head, opened his eyes and saw Murphy's face, all covered with blood, staring at him; and the muzzle of Murphy's pistol, veering round. He uttered a scream and, planting his elbows under his hips, he jerked backwards along the gutter. Murphy growled and made a sudden movement, raising himself a little to present his pistol and fire at the same moment. But just as he raised himself to fire, his head jerked upwards, the bullet fled from his gun harmlessly into the air above his head and he fell backwards, banging his skull against the gutter. He had been shot through the brain. He lay perfectly still.

The firing stopped. Soldiers were calling to one another from across the street. Dolan lay perfectly quiet looking at Murphy's body. Would he jump up now and raise his hands above his head? No. As soon as the thought of getting really into contact with the soldiers came into his head, his terror of them came back. He again realized that they were his enemies. A cold perspiration broke out all over his body and he crouched lower on to the roof, trying to push his body in through the slates, to hide himself. Then pressing against the roof, he lay still and shut his eyes.

Silence . . . a long silence. All was still.

Then there were footsteps on the roof behind him. He heard them and jumped up, waving his arms above his head. Then he fell on his knees and bent forward chattering and fluttering his clawing hands.

'Take me out of this. Take me out of this. I didn't fire. I didn't fire. He was mad. My wife, my wife. I declare to God I never fired. Two men on the stairs. Murphy is his name. Take me out of this.'

There were two of them there, peering over the ridge of the roof, five feet away from his face. Only their faces, their arms and their rifles were visible. Two cruel, cold faces, staring coldly at him. Gradually he saw the faces growing colder and more cruel, the lips curling into a snarl and the eyes narrowing. Then one man said: 'Let's give it to the bastard'.

They both fired point-blank into his head.

NEL BESTSELLERS

Crime

F.2131	GIRL IN A SHROUD	Carter Brown 3/6
F.2179	LAMENT FOR A LOUSY LOVER	Carter Brown 3/6
F.2185	DANCE OF DEATH	Carter Brown 3/6
F.1200	FAST WORK	Peter Cheyney 3/6
F.1291	DRESSED TO KILL	Peter Cheyney 3/6
F.1317	THE ADVENTURES OF JULIA	Peter Cheyney 3/6
F.2574	MURDER CAME LATE	John Creasey 5/–
F.2150	SECRET ERRAND	John Creasey 3/6
F.2485	DOWNPOUR	Ed. McBain 5/–
F.2365	TICKET TO DEATH	Ed. McBain 5/–
F.2341	MURDER MUST ADVERTISE	Dorothy L. Sayers 6/–
F.2317	STRONG POISON	Dorothy L. Sayers 5/–
F.2342	IN THE TEETH OF THE EVIDENCE	Dorothy L. Sayers 5/–
F.2316	CLOUDS OF WITNESS	Dorothy L. Sayers 5/–
F.2343	THE DOCUMENTS IN THE CASE	Dorothy L. Sayers 5/–
F.2315	WHOSE BODY?	Dorothy L. Sayers 5/–
F.2749	THE NINE TAILORS	Dorothy L. Sayers 6/–
F.2210	THE UNPLEASANTNESS AT THE BELLONA CLUB	Dorothy L. Sayers 5/–
F.2750	FIVE RED HERRINGS	Dorothy L. Sayers 6/–
F.2826	UNNATURAL DEATH	Dorothy L. Sayers 6/–

Fiction

F.2580	THE BEAUTIFUL COUPLE	William Woolfolk 7/6
F.2755	PAID SERVANT	E. R. Braithwaite 6/–
F.2289	THE SPANISH GARDENER	A. J. Cronin 5/–
F.2261	THE CITADEL	A. J. Cronin 7/6
F.2318	THE KEYS OF THE KINGDOM	A. J. Cronin 7/6
F.2752	THE HARRAD EXPERIMENT	Robert H. Rimmer 6/–
F.2429	PROPOSITION 31	Robert H. Rimmer 5/–
F.2427	THE ZOLOTOV AFFAIR	Robert H. Rimmer 5/–
F.2704	THE REBELLION OF YALE MARRATT	Robert H. Rimmer 6/–
F.2603	THE CARPETBAGGERS	Harold Robbins 12/6
F.2652	THE ADVENTURERS	Harold Robbins 14/–
F.2657	A STONE FOR DANNY FISHER	Harold Robbins 8/–
F.2654	NEVER LOVE A STRANGER	Harold Robbins 12/–
F.2653	THE DREAM MERCHANTS	Harold Robbins 12/–
F.2655	WHERE LOVE HAS GONE	Harold Robbins 10/–
F.2155	NEVER LEAVE ME	Harold Robbins 5/–
F.2327	THE SERPENT AND THE STAFF	Frank Yerby 7/6
F.2479	AN ODOUR OF SANCTITY	Frank Yerby 10/–
F.2326	BENTON'S ROW	Frank Yerby 7/6
F.2822	GILLIAN	Frank Yerby 8/–
F.2098	CAPTAIN REBEL	Frank Yerby 5/–
F.2421	THE VIXENS	Frank Yerby 7/6
F.2143	A WOMAN CALLED FANCY	Frank Yerby 5/–
F.2223	THE OLD GODS LAUGH	Frank Yerby 5/–

Romance

F.2152	TWO LOVES	Denise Robins 3/6
F.2153	THE PRICE OF FOLLY	Denise Robins 3/6
F.2154	WHEN A WOMAN LOVES	Denise Robins 3/6
F.2181	JONQUIL	Denise Robins 3/6
F.2182	LOVERS OF JANINE	Denise Robins 3/6
F.2241	THIS IS LOVE	Denise Robins 3/6
F.1355	DOCTOR OF MERCY	Elizabeth Seifert 3/6
F.2432	A BLAZE OF ARMS	Roger Fitzalan 5/–
F.2231	THE NEW DOCTOR	Elizabeth Seifert 4/–
F.2159	HARRIET HUME	Rebecca West 5/–
F.2523	CHANGE OF HEART	Jan Kennedy 5/–
F.2524	WOMAN OF SABLE	Jan Kennedy 5/–
F.2434	RAKEHELL ROCHESTER	Olivia Leigh 5/–
F.2435	THE FABULOUS BUCKINGHAM	Olivia Leigh 5/–

Science Fiction

F.2658	GLORY ROAD	Robert Heinlein 7/6
F.2659	STRANGER IN A STRANGE LAND	Robert Heinlein 10/-
F.2630	THE MAN WHO SOLD THE MOON	Robert Heinlein 6/-
F.2386	PODKAYNE OF MARS	Robert Heinlein 6/-
F.2449	THE MOON IS A HARSH MISTRESS	
F.2754	DUNE	

		Bentz Plagemann 5/-
F.		Lund/Ludlam 5/-
F.1084	THE GUNS OF AUGUST—AUGUST 1914	Barbara W. Tuchman 5/-

Western

F.2134	AMBUSH	Luke Short 3/6
F.2135	CORONER CREEK	Luke Short 3/6
F.2142	THE ALAMO	Lon Tinkle 3/6
F.2063	THE SHADOW SHOOTER	W. C. Tuttle 3/6
F.2132	THE TROUBLE TRAILER	W. C. Tuttle 3/6
F.2133	MISSION RIVER JUSTICE	W. C. Tuttle 3/6
F.2180	SILVER BUCKSHOT	W. C. Tuttle 3/6

General

F.2420	THE SECOND SEX	Simone De Beauvoir 8/6
F.2117	NATURE OF THE SECOND SEX	Simone De Beauvoir 5/-
F.2234	SEX MANNERS FOR MEN	Robert Chartham 5/-
F.2531	SEX MANNERS FOR ADVANCED LOVERS	Robert Chartham 5/-
F.1584	SEX AND THE ADOLESCENT	Maxine Davis 6/-
F.2136	WOMEN	John Philip Lundin 5/-
F.2333	MISTRESSES	John Philip Lundin 5/-
F.2382	SECRET AND FORBIDDEN	Paul Tabori 8/6
U.2366	AN ABZ OF LOVE	Inge and Sten Hegeler 10/6
F.2374	SEX WITHOUT GUILT	Albert Ellis Ph.D. 8/6
F.2511	SEXUALIS '95	Jacques Sternberg 5/-
F.2584	SEX MANNERS FOR SINGLE GIRLS	Dr. G. Valensin 5/-
F.2592	THE FRENCH ART OF SEX MANNERS	Dr. G. Valensin 5/-

Mad

S.3702	A MAD LOOK AT OLD MOVIES	4/6
S.3523	BOILING MAD	4/6
S.3496	THE MAD ADVENTURES OF CAPTAIN KLUTZ	4/6
S.3719	THE QUESTIONABLE MAD	4/6
S.3714	FIGHTING MAD	4/6
S.3613	HOWLING MAD	4/6
S.3477	INDIGESTIBLE MAD	4/6

- -

NEL P.O. BOX 11, FALMOUTH, CORNWALL

Please send cheque or postal order. Allow 9d. per book to cover postage and packing (Overseas 1/- per book).

Name..

Address ....

....

Title ....

(MARCH)